NIGHTS END

NIGHTS END

Urban Rain III

A NOVEL BY

David Dane Wallace

NIGHTS END
URBAN RAIN III

iUniverse books may be ordered through booksellers or by contacting:

iUniverse
1663 Liberty Drive
Bloomington, IN 47403
www.iuniverse.com
1-800-Authors (1-800-288-4677)

ISBN: 978-1-4917-8671-0 (sc)
ISBN: 978-1-4917-8670-3 (e)

Library of Congress Control Number: 2015921312

Print information available on the last page.

iUniverse rev. date: 01/15/2016

CONTENTS

CHAPTER I 1
CHAPTER II 31
CHAPTER III... 69

PART II
AND THE DEAD SHALL RISE 85

CHAPTER IV.. 103
CHAPTER V 123
CHAPTER VI.. 159

PART III
THE OTHER SIDE OF DARKNESS 177

Contents

CHAPTER ....
CHAPTER ....
CHAPTER ....

PART 2
INSTITUTIONAL INVESTMENT ....

FOR THE ETERNAL ENIGMA ... ... MONICA MEDEIROS ABBONA. I LOVE YOU NOW, FOREVER AND ALWAYS. YOU STILL HAUNT THE LONG AND WINDING CORRIDORS OF MY DREAMS EACH NIGHT AFTER I GO TO SLEEP. THERE IS ONLY ONE LIKE YOU, THERE WILL NEVER AGAIN BE ANOTHER. THERE ARE STILL TEARS ON MY PILLOW WHEN I AWAKE IN THE SHADOWS. REST IN PEACE BABY BUNNY. I'LL SEE YOU IN HEAVEN ... ...

THIS BOOK IS ALSO FOR MY TINY PRINCESS NIECE KATE. UNCLE VON LOVES YOU LITTLE ANGEL. I HOPE YOU WILL NEVER BE WITHOUT ME.

THIS BOOK IS ALSO DEDICATED TO MY BEST FRIEND AND CONSTANT COMPANION, MY DOGO, WARRIOR, THANKYOU FOR NEVER LEAVING MY SIDE BUDDY. DADDY LOVES YOU WITH ALL HIS HEART. I KNOW YOUR LIFE HASN'T BEEN EASY.

THIS BOOK IS ALSO FOR MY GRAND FATHER WALLACE, A GREAT WRITER, AND A PROUD MAN. R.I.P.

CHAPTER I

NIGHTMARES IN THE SUN by CONTROLLED DEMOLITION blasted from somewhere in the distance as Kate "The Gate" Shamrock stared at the epitaph on the head stone that sat at her knees … … … David "Von The Icon" Dane July, 15th, 1975 to July 28th, 2015. It was if the whole thing were a dream meant to jar her unconscious mind and scare her awake again, only reality had a different agenda.

"He never meant to leave you". Her Fathers consoling voice came from behind her.

"I know" Kate said rising from her squat on one knee. "It's just so hard to accept that he's gone".

The panel of sunlight below her had shifted and was now spread out across the bark of a cypress tree. Her Uncle had been dead for eleven days, and still no suspect had been arrested in his assassination, although the investigation was on going.

"This is free agent murder". Kate said. "Gunmen for hire".

"Yeah, one who uses poisonous arrows". Andrew exclaimed morbidly. "And in Ottawa of all places".

"Wasn't that neighbourhood one of Uncle Vons old stomping grounds"??

Andrew was nodding as an African native of average height appeared at his back. "Somerset and Wellington". The Wesley Snipes dead ringer proclaimed. He was suave and gifted in demeanour. He was also heavily accented.

"I'm sorry, I don't believe we've met". Andrew said in an un-assured voice.

The Ghana native gave a slight chuckle that was both charming and friendly. "Um Ray". He introduced shaking Andrews hand.

"Were you a friend of my Brothers"?? Andrew asked.

"He was my roommate". Ray proclaimed.

Andrews face had loosened. He knew who this guy was. "On Holmwood". Andrew clicked.

1

"Back in 1994". Ray laughed again with a nostalgic "He hee". "I respected your Brother. Mr. Magnum". Ray said. "That's what I used to call him, because that's who he looked like with his moustache".

"Yeah, Uncle Von did look a bit like Selleck with his moustache". Shamrock agreed, now flanked by her Mother who stood beside her. "He had a million nick names". Kate said fondly, still rubbing the tears from her eyes as they shimmered with emotion. "He was a hero, at least he was mine". She said.

"I heard about Mr. Magnums death on the news. My heart was broken". Ray said seriously. There was also a hint of anger on his palate.

They had at one time been inseparable, brothers from different Mothers. They had shared a million laughs during a very special era. One time a friend of Danes had driven Ray back home to Jane and Finch in Toronto where Ray had introduced him to a couple of Gang Members. The outcome was extremely memorable for its comedic value. Ray had returned to tell Dane in his deepest voice-"Ah mean, (Friends name omitted) cannot tell them that he has learning dis-a-bility. I told him, they are going to think that you are goofy, and they are going to murder us".

Rays remark had NOT been a slight on people with learning disabilities. It was the friend reporting it to a couple of full patch Crips that was so amusing. It had brought Dane to tears with laughter, even though he truly loved the friend in question.

"You lived with Uncle Von"?? Kate asked.

Ray was staring directly at the headstone now. "Um yup. Mr. Magnum". He repeated again. "You're his niece"?? Ray asked.

Kate was thinking that Ray must have been around the same age that her legendary Uncle had been. She also thought that women must have seen this guy as a smooth operator. He had it written all over him.

"Do you want a ride back into the city"?? Leilani Dane asked from behind her Daughter.

"No, it's okay. I can ride with Dad". She said.

"I'm Kate Shamrock". The Seasoned Fighter said extending her hand to Ray.

"Nice to meet you". He said. "Someone should find the person who did this and do something to him". Raymond exclaimed.

"Yeah no kidding". Shamrock agreed wiping a misfit tear from her cheek.

"Did you feed Warrior before you left"?? Kate asked her Father.

Warrior was David Danes Dogo. He was a big white friendly dog from the steps of Argentina whom Dane had acquired from The S.P.C.A. Most people were terrified of him, but in truth Warrior had one of the softest, sweetest, kindest hearts of any K-9 on the planet. He was to those who knew him well, a Prince.

"I did. He was hungry, so I fed him a little more than usual". Andrew responded.

"Okay, I am going to go now". Ray said. "I came to pay my respects to my Brother".

"It's okay, you can stay if you want". Andrew Dane invited.

"Nope, I have to leave, but I'll give you my phone number". He said breaking off the digits.

Andrew was programming them into his contact list now.

"Goodnight". Raymond said heading for his sports coup.

Monica-At the outset of the third installment in this series I want you to know that I miss you more than ever, like a sea of flames spreading out across the ocean. I want to tell you once more how much I love you, and will always love you. If it wasn't for you, there wouldn't be these books, nor this experience. This is the series that you inspired, and you are the star. My number one bunny, forever.

Von

Kate stepped out of her car into the fumes of the underground parkade of her building as a tall stranger approached her from behind. I'm Dee he said closing the distance between them. He explained that he was a friend of her Uncle Vons, and that he had been asked to come and see her in the event of his death.

"I knew your Uncle for two years before what happened. We were good friends. You probably never heard him mention me because I was a part of what he was involved with, the thing that got him killed".

"What got him killed"?? Shamrock asked with an emotional tremble in her voice, she had never heard anything about what led to her favorite Uncles demise.

Po, the giant panda that her Uncle Von had bought for her as a baby was sitting in the backseat of her car watching all of this, eyes wide and paws eternally raised forward as if reaching out for a hug. He had been her favorite toy as a child as well as her nightly companion. She had chosen to name him Po for no particular reason, it was simply his given name.

"I'm very sorry, I cannot tell you that because it could endanger your life". He explained. "He wanted me to come and see you in the event of his demise".

Dee spoke with an accent. Kate thought that he might have been Russian or Serbian, something eastern block. He was tall with roundish features and brownish hair. She thought that he must've been close to seven feet something, a man of formidable stature.

"Were you there when he died"?? She asked close to tears.

There were other vehicles entering the shadowy parkade now, one of which she had momentarily thought to be her Fathers, but she had been wrong. On the second level, there was a black van with tinted windows that's radio was squawking as it entered the darkness and then three or four basic looking cars. For a brief moment the womens kick boxing titlist felt a chill run the length of her spine for a reason that she could not discern.

"What's your last name Dee"?? The Irish Princess of the squared circle asked.

"I'm Dee Martine". (Pronounced-Marten). He said softly, not threatening. I'm humble and I'm pleased to meet you.

"How did you meet my Uncle Von"?? Kate "The Gate" Shamrock asked.

"We worked on something together. Your Uncle and I got involved with some bad people, people who kill. He was very worried about you and your Father. He wanted you to be safe. I know that he loved you endlessly. This is the picture of you that he kept in his wallet". Dee said unfolding a photo of the kickboxer with a blue hue in the background. There were a few water wrinkles, as if the photo had seen some rough weather. It was a photo that she remembered being taken in a boxing club after hours.

"Yeah, I remember when he took this". Kate said.

"I knew that he would have wanted you to have it. You really were the apple of his eye. He was the proudest Uncle that I've ever seen". The big man said looking away momentarily as if half expecting to see something.

"Yeah, that I know". Kate said.

"There was blood in the street when he died". Martine stated. "At least that's what the papers said. I intend to avenge your Uncle. He shouldn't be a dead man. He had just turned forty".

"I was there when he blew out his candles". Shamrock reminisced emotionally turning her gaze in the direction of the blue vapour shadows of the underground parking lot.

"He never mentioned you, but I guess there was a reason for that. I don't know what he was working on. Was this the bi product of something that he knew. Uncle Von was an author, a boxer and a street legend. I've never known him to be anything else. I'm sorry". Kate said.

"There were other things". Martine said seeming to drop tone for a moment.

"He was a good man". He said.

Just then another car entered the parkade and crawled slowly past them. The driver seemed to take cognisance of Shamrock as he thumbed a button on his sun visor.

"I'd invite you in but I don't know you". Kate said.

"No, I understand. You're Vons niece. He wouldn't have expected anything less. I'll leave you my cell number in case you need to reach me. It's … …"

When Andrew Dane walked through the front door and into his living room WARRIOR trotted up to greet him. He was a warm hearted friendly dog who was very emotional about anyone leaving or abandoning him, and WARRIOR was in his own right, an angel.

"Hi buddy". Andrew Dane said petting the adorable Dogo on the head.

"Roof". WARRIOR responded, his tail wagging furiously to the degree that there was a fear that he might break it off.

"I just gave him some food, the Hypoallergenic kind". Leilani remarked holding a dish in one hand as she dried it with another. "He likes it better than the other stuff, but something tells me he'd rather have Lasagne".

"I don't doubt it". Andrew said draping his blue blazer over the edge of the couch, he had taken the day off work to spend time with Kate, and to visit his Brothers grave.

There was for a brief moment a silence, and then the phone rang. Kate was on the other end, a bit breathy. She told her Father right away about her meeting with Dee and what he had told her.

"What he was working on"?? Andrew asked bewildered. "What the hell does that mean"??

"I don't know". Kate answered reaching for a mug at the same time. It read-Blond Girls And Barbell Curls. It had once belonged to her Uncle. Some sort of Gym token.

"Since when did your Uncle become James Bond, because that's what it sounds like"!!??

"VON, JAMES VON". Kate said holding onto the mug with both hands and smiling.

WARRIOR groaned from a few feet behind his adopted Uncle, this was either an expression of dissatisfaction or a prelude to him leaving the house in search of other residence.

"Okay, okay, listen. I have to take WARRIOR out before he marks his territory on the rug". Andrew proclaimed trolling around the living room in search of WARRIORS elusive leather dog leash.

"Ciao". Kate said on the other end.

WARRIOR The Adorable DOGO had not had an easy life, he had been made a resident of The S.P.C.A. and Animal Rescue over and over again by cruel owners who could have given a damn about him despite his handsome appearance, heart of gold, and incredibly pronounced class. He was beyond that which deserved reference to as a "Good Dog, and kind, loving animal". If you met one K-9 in this lifetime who would put his whole heart on display for you, then it was WARRIOR.

"Let's go for a walk". Kate said hooking WARRIOR up to his leash.

WARRIOR stood up groaning pleasantly at the realization that he was about to be taken for his walk by one of his favorite people in the world. It was high noon, and it had been three hours since breakfast. No more leaning over the edge of the couch watching talk shows and sit coms. It was time to hit the streets and all of the scents and free treats that went with them.

Kate stepped into the cool morning sunshine with WARRIOR THE WONDER DOG two steps ahead of her. He was a big dude she registered once again. He looked like a Pit Bull, but was in all actuality, a DOGO ARGENTINIAN, a rare breed of K-9 here in Montreal, and a rare gem to have been found at The S.P.C.A. Her Uncle had truly been very proud of WARRIOR, and boasted constantly of his many special traits.

WARRIOR-This is where Daddy whoops the DOG FUCK out of your former owners for the way they treated you. As long as there is air in my body you will NEVER, EVER have to endure being left at The S.P.C.A., A Dog Rescue, or on The Street, ever again, and I know how that hurt your heart. I can't imagine the cold storage shed in place of a soul that your former Parents must have had. Daddy loves you baby, not just half hearted, but with his whole heart. You are the most special K-9 in the entire world, I only wish you could have known HUNTER because the two of you would have been best friends. THEY-YOUR FORMER OWNERS-ARE NOTHING, AND YOU ARE SOMETHING. Your pictures will be all over this book that will be sold around the world. I hope that one day your former owners see this Book, so they will know what a great friend and an angel that they lost in you.

Again, I LOVE YOU WARRIOR, NOW AND ALWAYS, FOREVER!!!!!!

Daddy

"I think that my Brother was involved in something, I don't know what or why, but I want to bring closure to this issue". Andrew said standing opposite Leilani who was sitting on the arm rest of the couch listening intently word for word to her husbands pain. Andrew had endured a lot, and she did not know how much more he could take. It didn't take much to understand that all of this had taken its toll on him, not to mention that it had torn their little girls heart to shreds.

The Funeral for Von "The Icon" had been a huge event that was broadcast all over T.V. and multi-media world wide. There had been people there from across the globe that had attracted International Attention.

Phil Collins had come out of retirement to sing Long Long Way To Go from his 1980's album-NO JACKET REQUIRED. Nickelback had also been in attendance to perform their hit single-LULLABY. There were authors, movie stars, models, Boxing Champions, Pro Wrestlers, Gang members, The Ontario Street Originals, and even a bouquet of flowers from a friend of his who worked for a branch of his publishing company in South East Asia.

"I have to go get the dry cleaning. Do you want anything to eat"?? Andrew asked reaching for the back of his neck with two fingers as he twisted his head around.

"I had a sandwich earlier so I'm not that hungry". Leilani said lifting a magazine from a fold in the couch and placing it on the table.

Andrew reached for a set of keys and headed for the door. He had spent his life watching his legendary Brother endure, now he had to watch him die. The trade off hardly seemed fair, and the bitterness that it had instilled in him was palpable. This wasn't something that Andrew would let go of. There would be payment in full by those responsible, a debt that would bare the burden of full collection, no agent required.

It still haunted him that Lilly had gone to Heaven followed by his Brother, both long before their time. He hoped they were together now, and that they'd resolved things. Lilly Chicoine had been the love of his Brothers life, bar none. There had never been a woman who had possessed his Brothers mind, heart, and soul so completely even as many women as there were in and out of his Brothers life over the years. Her name had always brought tears to his eyes after she died.

Outside in the parking lot that over looked the ocean Andrew took the salt silvered air into his nostrils. It was warm outside, hardly common for this late month of the year. "Thanks for watching it for me". The husky Andrew Dane said to the parking attendant who had just turned over his keys.

"No problem Boss". Warren said as Andrew put a hundred in his hand.

Andrews sports car purred into neutral as it sped out of the parking lot and headed onto the road that over looked The St. Lawrence River.

SEXXXY EDDY climbed out of the ring to a round of cheers as he celebrated the defeat of another opponent. He didn't know if he'd ever be able to do it again after the tragedy in Glens Falls New York and the death of a Wrestler named Gabriel Sykes. It had been a freak accident that no one could have seen coming. It was the set up for a Pile Driver on the concrete when Eddy had been blindsided by another Wrestler who had thrown him off balance and caused Eddy and his opponent whom he had hardly known to sail sideways into the guard rail. The blow had caused trauma to Sykes brain that had later led to his death at a local medical facility. The event had altered Eddys life. He had felt so badly that he was sending monthly cheques to Gabriels widow, Tamantha, and then ten days later Von had been found dead in a shady area of Ottawa with an arrow of all things, through his heart. Eddy had prepared a eulogy and read it at his friends funeral. It had brought forth an emotional response from the crowd as both were CANADIAN NATIONAL HERO'S.

"You're words were beautiful". Kate Shamrock had later commented.

"Eddy, you want one of these"?? A nearby ring hand asked offering Eddy Dorozowsky an Evian water.

Eddy took it and kept walking toward the dressing rooms. The Fans had made signs offering their condolences over the Sykes incident as well as David Danes death, one of them read-WE STILL LOVE YOU EDDY, IT WASN'T YOUR FAULT. It was a sentiment that had brought tears to Dorozowskys eyes. Another read VON "THE ICON", MY IMMORTAL, CANADA'S HERO FOREVER … … … … ALL OUR LOVE!!!!

This was probably why he'd become a Wrestler, even if he didn't know it. The love of these people, their emotions, their friendship, as corny as that might have sounded in todays Pro Wrestling climate full of popular heels, nonetheless it was true. Look at the love they'd shown him in the wake of The Sykes incident. No one would ever disrespect Wrestling Fans in Eddys presence ever again, not if they didn't want to get dropped like a bundle of cradled cinder blocks.

"I hope you watched me wrestle tonight". Eddy said gesturing toward an invisible sky. He was speaking to Von, his late Brother from another Mother. They would never fight in the street together again nor close a bar with their jokes and stories. Eddy hoped that whatever bastard killed his friend would eternally burn. Forever!!

"This yours"?? Another Pro Wrestler asked as Eddy returned to the dressing room. The five hundred pound mammoth was holding Eddys jacket in his grip.

"Yeah, that's mine". The Sex Symbol said as he reached into his kit bag and removed a pair of sun visors that used to belong to Von. "I'm gonna make them sorry that this ever happened one day buddy". Eddy said to the spirit of his friend. It was too much nightmare, too much loss all at once. There seemed to be no end to the tragedy that just kept spilling forth.

At a bar later that night Eddy signed autographs for fans prefaced with the words-R.I.P. V.T.I. and G.S. a nod of respect to those who had passed. There were tears welled in his eyes as he handed the paper, pictures, and pens back to his fans. He was a face, but instead he felt like the heel (Wrestling for bad guy). He wondered how much of his emotion the blue room full of fans had seen. It would take him years to forgive himself for killing another Wrestler, accident or not. He was supposed to protect his opponent in the ring contrary to the belief of the few marks (Kayfabe for Wrestling Fans) who hadn't been smartened up or were too young to know the difference. This was two more heart breaks in a series of many. Prior to the two aforementioned tragedies Eddy had lost an older sister to an illness, it had been the most emotional tribulation of his life. There was no getting over that, and had Eddy had his way, he would have had it been himself who passed instead of the little sister whom he loved with all his heart and considered to be an angel. Her name was Alexandra, and she was in Heaven.

"Love you Alexandra" Eddy said kissing a photo of his lost sibling. "I'll bet you're wearing a halo". He said of his older sister. "Rest in peace".

EDDY-I want to thank you for appearing in three out of four of my books, and for always being a terrific sport. Growing up as a Wrestling Fan, I'm proud to have a Wrestler in my books. You always show up on time to sign off and never utter a word of complaint. I love you Brother.
Regards,
Von "The Icon",
Cheers!!!

Kate Shamrock rounded the corner into the night in her sleek black sports coup. There were tears in her eyes as she fondly remembered the Uncle she'd lost. In so many ways he was a hero to her, not the least of which was constantly being her sounding board or shoulder to cry on. The Immortal Von "The Icon" would never be forgotten. "Kill you motherfucker". She said of the shadowy figure with cross bow in her head, poised, ready to assassinate her legendary Uncle from atop a low standing building.

"This is what you do to Canadian hero's. Your days are fucking numbered jack off". She thought aloud as she put the car in another gear.

There were trees ahead now and a drop off that she narrowly missed as an oncoming car swerved to avoid her. There was no one in this world who had inspired her like her one of a kind heroic uncle. He had been a legitimate bad ass and a hero to millions. She would make this cross bow wielding fuck spit his tongue out on the ground as she had made Jacky Hannah pay for killing Lilly Chicoine. This would be one killers worst dream, an all out, full on, nightmare. He would pay for everything that he had done.

"Hello. Hey". Kate said answering her ring tone. "I should be home in a couple of hours. I have someone that I have to pass by and see first … … … … yep, yep. I'll tell Donovan that you said "Hi". Kate finished hanging up on her Mother.

"Me Gate". Donovan greeted as Kate entered the sweat streaked shadows of her coaches tin roofed boxing club. "It's good of yah to come by and see a lonely old man".

"Donovan please, I'll bet you're as much of a stud today as you were at twenty".

"Whoever said I was a stud at twenty"??

"Are you still taking me to see CREED"??

"CREED, that's the film about Apollo Creeds son, the one that Stallones in"??

"That's the one. So is it a date"??

"Indeed it is". Donovan said taking Kate by the arm and leading her toward the office that sat at an extreme corner of the club. You trained fighters here, you didn't entertain, or socialize, and it seemed certain that it wasn't fit for anyone who saw themselves as being from an upper or even middle class echelon of society. It was not for the faint of heart or weak of mind. These were the poor and hungry who had come to fight, to move up from the gutter by slugging their way out. This was the sweat box, urban hungry. This was a building that had seen it's day many, many years ago, a relic, like its head coach.

"I love you Donovan". Kate said of her trainer.

"Oh, and I love you that much more me Gate. Why, if it wasn't for you, I'd likely be so deep in the ground that they'd need an archaeologist to dig up me remains".

"Never". Kate said flipping the light switch inside of the office and sitting down.

"Can I ask yah something me Gate, because I know this is a sensitive issue for you. Have they made any progress in finding your Uncles killer"?? Donovan asked polishing his coffee mug with a rag.

"No, but I met a friend of his, or someone who claims to know him".

Donovan looked bewildered, stirring at this revelation. There were boxing gloves hanging over a rack behind him alongside a towel and a sparring helmet. "How did you meet this person?? I'm assuming it's a lad".

"He was in the parkade below my building. He's seven feet. I've never seen a bigger monster in my life". She said of her new acquaintance that could over shadow The Statue Of Liberty.

"Well does this monster have a name"?? Donovan Alexander O Riley asked pouring himself a cup of Coffee from a flask. His curiosity had been over whelmed, and his weathered old face reflected it.

"Dee Martine". Shamrock responded.

Kate heard the door creak at her back as she turned to see a sliver of light from a crack in the entrance at the front of the club. There was no sound after that.

"Can I help ye"?? Donovan called from the brightly lit office, but no response came.

"It's just me, I was hoping I could find Kate here". Andrew said from the engulfing absence of light of the outer club. It was in his heart now, with the sweat, fever and intense passion left behind in the air. It reminded him of his Brother, and what a nightmare that losing him had been. Every so often he felt compelled to tears, and this was one of those times. They had grown up in the small city of Halifax, Nova Scotia and then branched out to other parts of the country, Andrew to Calgary, Toronto, and Montreal and Von to Ottawa, Vancouver, Toronto, and finally Montreal where his greatest legacies existed among the brewery drenched air of the east end, a neighbourhood and a community that he'd made famous world wide. He had made a name for himself on those streets, both he and the iconic Lilly "Bad To The Bone" Chicoine. Their story was now the stuff of legend.

"Why are there tears in your eyes, or is it for the same reason that there are tears in mine"?? Kate asked ...

Ray walked into the living room of his expensive condo wading through an ocean of memories of his fallen friend. He had been up the better part of the night talking to his pal Kofi on the phone as he went through the things that he had to get off his chest. All his life, Ray had never let his friends go un avenged. He would find the man or men who did this and make them pay. "Um yup, they will be here any moment from now". Ray said as he spit blood into the sink and closed his cellphone. "Fuck them". Ray said to no one. He had been on the phone with his girlfriend and was now waiting for two of his buddies to come over. "I can't fuckin focus on any ting until I lay these mother fuckers to rest". Ray thought aloud of his invisible adversaries.

Ray had spent years and years living at Jane and Finch in Toronto making himself a favorite among scores of gorgeous dames as well as some very dangerous gang members, and his reputation proceeded him wherever he went, junior gun men or seasoned mobsters, they all loved Ray for who he was, and for what he stood for.

For a moment he saw himself standing in the living room of their apartment on Holmwood in Ottawa.

There was a grin on his face as he jokingly told his housemate "I am sweet, sweet, black man" ... ...

"That's why I gave you the apartment". Von replied in the character of the smart ass that he was.

They had many a good times together. They had been the best of friends, like brothers, and to their upstairs neighbours who held all night parties, they had been a holy terror. Ray chuckled as he recalled one night where he and his friend Mr. Magnum had confronted a group of Foot Ball Players who were making a racket above them. "Ah mean, you can't make this kind of noise. It is after midnight". Ray had warned them. Von had a tire iron in his hand, and a terse expression on his face. The combination of the two had gotten their neighbours to turn down their music.

Then he remembered another evening when Von had been dancing face to face with Rays then girlfriend Claudette. The song was HEY MR. D.J. by Zhane, it had been a fun night and the three had been thick as thieves. They were all great friends.

13

"Whoever you are that did this, I don't know who the fuck you are, but I am going to make you pay". Ray said with lethal sincerity in his voice, and it was a promise, and a threat that he intended to keep.

"We wanna know who you're working for". Detective Gable of The Ottawa Carleton Regional Police Department demanded of the gorgeous former dancer turned call girl who sat before him.

"It's like I already told you". The strawberry blond with the enhanced lips, big breasts and smug demeanour responded "I don't work for anyone. Von was my friend, that's it. We walked into that bar to grab a couple of drinks, well, I was gonna drink, Von was gonna down something else cause he doesn't drink alcohol. When we got outside there was somebody waiting for him with a cross bow. I just saw the shadow". She said taking drawn out puffs from her smoke.

"You didn't see anything?? You never saw a face because you would've been awfully close to that roof top. This is a prominent Canadian citizen, a national hero. We're gonna find out who did this to him and they're going away". Gable promised encircling the narrow white table that sat in the centre of the room. He was an older Detective who had spent over thirty five years doing what he did. He had worked narcotics for a time before that and then moved over to homicide.

"Look, we know who you are. You set up Michael Bradford underneath a bridge eight years ago over a drug debt. You've already got that working against you. Now if you had anything to do with this you better start talking before we prove it on our own and decide to charge you with Conspiracy to Commit. That's twenty years".

"I didn't set up anyone". Cindy Prescott maintained tipping her cigarette into a blue ash tray. "You motherfuckers are all the same, you always wanna pin a case on someone whether they did anything or not".

Gable was frowning now, his eye brows furrowed. He did not like this sleazy, disreputable woman with her disrespectful attitude and cool, smug demeanour. As far as he was concerned she should be locked up tonight on suspicion alone. "How'd you meet David Dane"?? Gable asked furthering his bad standing with the tramp who sat before him.

"Didn't you hear me the first time?? I used to dance at a club in Hull that Dane and one of his buddies frequented".

"But I don't suppose you know the name of the friend". Winston Gable continued. He felt like trash talking her but he held his tongue, she made him sick as soon as you got passed her looks. She was a viper, fuckin cunt.

"Nope. I never spoke to him". She said blowing smoke out the side of her expensive lips.

"Hmm". Gable said shrugging it off. "What time did you get to the club"?? He pressed with his left fist pressed into his hip.

"I don't know. I already told you this. It was eight, nine, I'm not sure". She said expelling some more smoke from her surgery site.

"You guys talk to anyone over there, a bartender, anyone"??

"Nope, just him and me. I was gonna take him home with me, but Von got shot".

Gable shot her a disapproving glance, her arrogance was thicker than Gables gun holster. He had seen few women with her penchant for narcissism. What a total fucking self absorbed bitch, beyond her appearance, which was considerable, she had not a single redeeming quality. There had been a plethora of egos in this room over time, but few as formidable as this womans. Two years ago they had arrested a woman for taking one of her husbands guns from a rack and killing her entire Family. She had been as remorseless a killer as Gable had ever seen, but even her attitude paled in comparison to this womans.

"Why did you kill your three children"?? Gable had asked her, and then she had sat there with her cigarette the same way. "Because their crying got on my nerves, I'd be trying to fuck my boyfriend and they wouldn't shut up".

Gable had wanted to toss her in an eight by ten prison cell and throw away the key, eventually, he had gotten his wish. She was now serving four consecutive life sentences. Some of the trash that walked through this door made Gable want to drive home and get in the shower. It never ceased to amaze Winston how some people could kill their loved ones with a sickening impunity that seemed to serve the lowest denominator of the human soul.

"What"?? Winston yelled into his cell phone as he stormed out into the corridor without excusing himself. "Who the fuck got her Danny Green"?? He demanded of the desk sergeant who was at the other end of the line.

Danny Green was one of Ottawas most prominent criminal attorneys, a maverick, and in the eyes of the cops, a criminal freeing Satan.

"Fine, send him down". Gable reluctantly agreed.

Five minutes later a smug, arrogant expensively dressed Danny Green entered the interrogation room where Gable and Prescott were now seated amidst an uneasy tension.

"Please leave my client and I alone for a moment". Green demanded giving off an air that would have made God himself feel inferior, but it did not phase Gable who had dealt with many a saucy defence lawyer in his own time on the force. "Fine". He agreed tapping three of his fingers one after another against the table top before standing up. "I'll be outside". He said dismissing himself from the black room with only a single burning lamp.

"So, I'll bet you wanna get out of here". Green said when they were finally alone.

Cindy was smiling now. "Who sent you"?? She asked, bewildered.

"Jonathan Dane did". Danny Green said with a wicked smirk on his face.

"If it brought you no peace to know who I was then why did you ask". Cyril Mathews asked the path in front of him. That's what they were, a bad dream that he'd put together himself. They were suicide, acquisition and fire, deranged simply by existence. Each face amongst the gathering shadows before him was willing to die, willing to give up hope, willing to do whatever he asked on a moments notice if he so requested or so desired. Many of those that were "The Path" or that comprised it had spent time in psychiatric wards or had done on and off stints in suicide hospitals. Death or its inherent concept was nothing extravagant to them. He had been their leader revealing who and what he really was bit by bit. Now, gathered here in the basement of this old two story Victorian mansion they were everything and all that The Devil or Jonathan Dane could have asked for. Jonathan was an innate sadist wicked to the very words that he spoke. He may have been raised on Jesus and had at one time been a Christian altar boy but had long since burnt that cattle to the earth. Inside, in places that darkness spoke about he had become a man of another cloth even severing the throat of his own wife who was still on life support. This was immeasurable wickedness and perseverance of purest fire that had made Jonathan a vile if not immeasurably evil human being. He had never been a kind man, but only gave the appearance of kindness to those that he wanted to shed dishonest light upon. He was inside sick and twisted to his throat. He had orchestrated the kill of his own son from a rooftop in the nations capital a hop, skip, and a jump from Parliament. What Jonathan Dane most enjoyed was the suffering of others. It was misery and pain that served as the backbone of Jonathan Danes ensemble in life, and he lived to bask in the hurt of those he should have loved.

"This is Dr. Peter Claven". Cyril Mathews introduced wandering toward a far corner of the shadowy room full of alcoves and sinister dimensions where he had sliced a five year olds throat only two days and one night ago. "It's Dr. Claven who brought most of you to me". Mathews proclaimed as a chorus of morbid sighs rose from the blackness that engulfed the group whom Claven had brought together as one unity.

"I don't want you to scream when you see what I did to the child". Mathews said readying the video footage that he'd shot with an infrared lens. It was of he, the five year old being coaxed into a corner as he shook his head, and then the knife came out from somewhere beside Mathews who was wearing silver flesh tone and an evil grimace. In a few moments the focus of the camera shifted away into another corner and then came back to what Mathews was doing. There were a few low moans from the room and then a shriek from the footage that was no older than six. After that you could see nothing except the boys fluid on the camera lens.

"You're going to do the same for me". Mathews said spreading a hypnotic cackle over the room. It was as if it belonged in more than one place, somehow projected. He wanted to fuck now, it was all over inside him. Killing and seeing his own work turned him on.

"I want her virginity". He said to one of the youngest girls in the flock who was lighting a candle now.

"Disrobe Helen for me Margo". He commanded and watched as one of the female elders did as she was told.

Mathews was removing his robe now to expose himself in the glow of the candle that she had set for him. He had a full blown erection, and his minions, his followers acted as his audience. Kill and receive. Tonight, they were holding hands with Satan. The virgin was looking into his eyes now, giving herself to him both in spirit and sexually. There were distant sounds from somewhere, as if from a water fall among wind chimes.

"Give yourself to me young one". He said as he spread himself out on top of her … … … …

Andrew Dane reached for his Daughters hand. "I love you". He said speaking to her image in darkness, and then she vanished into nights hold and he couldn't find her. She had disappeared, completely evaporated amongst the silhouette of branches and darkness that seemed to exist beyond whatever window, beneath a strange and moonless sky. It seemed as if somehow he was crying, needle pointing tears in a whispery wind. Kate was all his love, all that engulfed every single corner of his heart like an angel without wings. "I still see you Dad". She said from past the reach of his vision. He was in a park searching for her, turning one corner after another becoming one with the sighing winds, and then somewhere out of nowhere came Lilly Chicoine who seemed to be trying to point him in the right direction, as if she knew and understood his plight.

Andrew looked at her emotionally for a moment and nodded, as if trying to tell her that he was sorry for her loss. Lilly nodded understandingly.

Then he walked further into this park like cemetery where he ran into the image of his Brother breathing, looking toward him and pointing. His eyes were wet now. He missed David, and was haunted by the fact that his Brother was gone. The sighing, breathing, tormented winds shifted in the tree tops again before he lifted his hand to his sleeping eyes. There, before him, in a casket was his precious Daughter with a visible knife wound to her neck. "LET GO"!!! He heard her shout in his head, and then he woke screaming in his darkened bedroom.

Kate Shamrock stepped once to her left before executing a martial arts style standing side kick. "Alright Gloria, you try it". She urged the student who stood in the ring before her. Gloria was an off duty Police Officer who had come to learn all she could from the seasoned Shamrock who as a womans champion had earned more gold than almost any other female titlist in history. Just last month Kate had flown to L.A. to have dinner with Ronda Rousey and had subsequently also bumped into THE ROCK who had given her his phone number.

"Okay, but push when you step into it". Shamrock, all dressed in black said. There was a picture of Von "The Icon" on the wall behind her.

"Good, now stand back and try again". She said turning around to see the seven foot something Dee standing in the wings behind her. "Hey, nice to see you". She said slightly out of breath and off key.

"I think so, yeah". The monster said jestingly. "You have your Uncles desire to win. It's in your eyes. You're VON "THE ICONS" niece ... ...

"And who the fuck does that make you". A voice challenged from a number of feet behind The massive Goliath who could have frightened a Dinosaur.

Dee turned fully around to see Ray staring him in the face, no blinders on and taking him all in. "Mm hmm. You don't look like a friend of Mr. Magnums". Ray said boldly to the giant who towered over him like a guard from the gates of Hell.

"And you don't look like much". Dee said coldly with a scowl beginning to shadow his eyes.

"Why don't you come outside then and see". Ray invited without flinching.

"Okay, guys, let's like relax and not kill each other here". Shamrock said jumping out of the ring to get between them.

For the first time Kate had seen Dee look really mean while Ray simply looked absolutely, a hundred percent serious.

"You're an infection". Dee said.

"I'm what"?? Ray responded. "If I see you outside somewhere I am going to kill you, for sure".

"Okay, okay, you guys, just relax". Kate said standing between the two men who were about to tear each other apart. She had been in a thousand and one of these situations with her legendary Uncle Von, this simply, was one more.

Dee poured over the much shorter Ray who was heart and fire, unafraid. "He's a big mouth, but I shut it later on". Vons former flat mate threatened, he did not like this interloper who seemed to be a total jerk.

"Aright, whadya you guys say we grab a shake across the street at MC Donalds"?? Kate asked slightly out of breath in this predicament, then she thought better of it. If the three of them exited the building there might be a fight, and again, she'd be playing referee. God, she wished that her Uncle was here.

"I'm going to leave". Dee said slowly backing toward the door.

"Mmm hmm". Ray responded, his eyes never leaving his adversaries.

"Thank God that's over". Shamrock commented.

"I don't think your Uncle would like him". Ray said.

Monica- I love you, as each day passes, I miss you that much more. I am going through an awful time in my life right now. I am being psychologically tortured beyond anything that you could ever imagine by almost everyone around me. I miss the shadowy days and nights that we used to prowl O Street together of cuddle on the mattress in front of the T.V. and watch movies. I'll never forget those moments, my years with you, our years, were the most special of my life. Ye know all the girls who work O Street now call you "THE LEGEND", and you earned it. You are the most fearless female that I've ever known. No one, and I mean, no one exemplifies hard core the way that you do. You are The Princess of that genre. I try so hard sometimes to bring back that flavor, that ambience, that these streets once possessed, but without you, it's gone. It died with you. You died in an execution chamber made of lines and concrete, but your name, and your story, will go down in history. You are a Canadian Hard Core Legend. They broke the mold when they made you.

All my love, always,

Von

WARRIOR trotted cheerfully across the kitchen floor of The Danes condo, he had been anxiously anticipating his afternoon walk and now here it was. Leilani hooked WARRIOR to his leash and headed for the front door which was approximately fifteen feet ahead of her. It was just past three p.m. and she was expecting Andrew to walk through the door at any moment, carrying his designer brief case.

"Ready to go for your walk"?? Leilani asked turning toward the handsome and adorable Dogo Argentinian who had been bounced from place to place in his life. It had not been easy on him, but WARRIOR had fought the odds and persevered despite all of the adversity that had been thrown his way. His journey had gone from one owner to another to The Rescue to The S.P.C.A., to the late Von "The Icon" to she, Andrew and Kate who treated WARRIOR as if he were her child, he had even gotten to sit ringside during a couple of her fights in a V.I.D. booth for VERY IMPORTANT DOGO!!!

WARRIOR had been the apple of David Danes eye. Dane had taken WARRIOR for a two and three hour walk each day always making sure he was fed, had his pills, and was well taken care of. He had been extremely special to him. In many ways WARRIOR was a living teddy bear or an 85ib. baby. He had a big heart and loved to be cuddled. He had for a long time slept next to Dane who would cuddle up to him as though he were just that, a teddy bear. WARRIOR was a very special animal indeed.

"Roof". WARRIOR said excitedly, ready to go. He wore a silver chain around his neck with a pink/purple clover shaped dog tag. He was always a popular hit wherever he went with his short white fur and gigantic jaw. He had large brown eyes that seemed to always express love and happiness, and indeed he WARRIOR was a happy dog.

Dane had expressed once that WARRIOR was such a hit with women that he should dress him as a pimp. The image had been funny, WARRIOR leaning over the edge of David Danes couch wearing a black hat with a round rim and a matching silk shirt.

WARRIOR was a beautiful dog that the world loved, and despite his lethal looking appearance he had the heart and spirit of an angel. He had attended Von "The Icons" Funeral dressed in a white suit and had even cried. He had been very emotional.

Leilani stepped out into the sunshine with WARRIOR snug on his black, leather leash. He was busy sniffing a tree trunk now.

"Did you find something special"?? She asked as she observed Andrew parking his car across the street.

WARRIOR gave no response, nose still on the hunt.

"I ordered some Chinese. It should be here in half an hour". Andrew Dane said folding his work blazer across his left forearm. He wore a white dress shirt over grey steel colored pressed pants. Most of his wardrobe was worth thousands, a tailor made line.

"I was gonna take WARRIOR for his walk. Save some for me and I'll put it in the fridge for later on". Leilani said. "He needs his walk".

"I thought we were gonna eat together. Alex might come by as well but I guess it can wait".

"Is this place any good"?? Leilani asked.

"Better than the last". Andrew said staring across the street at the parked Mazda and the man with the sun glasses who sat behind its wheel. "Who the fuck is that"?? Andrew asked squinting in the glare. No sooner were the words off his lips then the man put the car into gear and sped away from the curb.

Brandy stepped onto the sidewalk into the east ends dead heat. She had been born and raised on Ontario Street from childhood and now ran a business here. It had been hard at first, but eventually her establishment had become a success raking in loads of cash from the regulars who came to purchase the assortment of baked goods, squares and health drinks etc that her establishment boasted. It also didn't hurt that Brandy was a looker who attracted rounds of attention from most of the local studs, one of whom had been Von "The Icon" who would drop in several times a week before taking his dog WARRIOR for his daily walk. It had been on those sticky afternoons that she and Ontario Streets Legend had become close friends often sitting down to share an ice cream and talk. There was also a mutual attraction between the incredible black haired blue eyed sex symbol and her legendary customer. Von also appreciated Brandys polite flirtatious demeanour and attractive character that calmed him when his nerves were on edge.

Now here alone Brandy thought of her famous client and what attending his funeral had been like. She had cried a thousand tears and said her goodbyes at the wake. She never thought in a million years that being close to him would lead to a bouquet of flowers and a closed casket as a final act. He had been a good man never for a second betraying who he was for anyone be it friend or foe. Fuckin bastards, whoever was behind the arrow gun deserved worse than what they had done to her friend. They would fry if she had her way. In her minds eye she saw herself deep kissing Von against the wall of her store one night after hours as the two sunk to the floor in each others embrace.

"Close your eyes". Von whispered before he kissed her full on. Now that moment seemed so surreal to her, as if evaporated into a hidden twilight, one with many shadows.

"I've done bad things" Von said. "I've tried to atone for who I am a thousand times over".

"How bad"?? The sexy bomb shell asked, her gorgeous blue eyes sparkling in the night.

Brandy was what Dane called, Gothic Intense, her combination of jet black hair, pouty lips and sexy personality had immediately attracted his attention. She was a superstar.

"That's what you should learn how to do. Make Gothic shakes. There's something to shoot for".

Brandy gazed across at her friend for a moment before wiping a streak of strawberry from his lips. "That's all that you like about me"?? She asked coyly.

"You have other talents". He said leaning across the bench and kissing her.

"I wanted him to die, at least that's what was in my sights. Do you have any idea what it's like to be a Father and hate your sons fuckin guts?? I watched him and all of his fame and I couldn't stomach it. He was nothing but trouble, right from day one. I want them to spit on his grave right where the epitaph is". Jonathan Dane said sitting in the confines of a limousine surrounded by members of The Path who sat upright in his presence. I would've paid ten goddamn times as much to have him killed".

"I would've done it for you". Derek Muldiva said in a weak temperate voice. He had joined The Path only a month ago and was now eager to please his sinister, affluent leader who funded Cyril Mathews. "I killed a dog and a woman once. It was at Cyrils request, and he allowed me to keep the womans hand". Muldiva said.

There was motion outside before someone came to the window behind which Jonathan Dane sat and handed him a phone. "Hello". He answered in a strong voice. There was static at the other end for a moment. "Oh". Dane said to whomever he was speaking to. "I'll do that. I'll have to call you back". He said as the car made a right turn into an alley way and parked below a tall fire escape.

"This is Billy Turner". Derek introduced as a slender black haired male with large tattoos entered the car. "Hi", Billy said enthusiastically. "Can I do a hit here"?? He asked looking over at Jonathan who wore a black cloak over grey dress pants and a silk shirt.

There was something very cold about Jonathan, Billy registered, like a Sociopath turned sociopathic. Jonathan reflected not a single discernible trace of human emotion, stoic in presentation and single mindedly evil. This is the way he had lived, and this all in all was the way he would die, for Jonathan Dane did not care about people, and understood nothing of kindness.

Had there been a time ever, when he was good or decent, simply was gone like smoke rising from distant stacks into a limitless night. In his childhood, as an altar boy, he had via his own action mocked the very cloth that he purported to exemplify, always enjoying the pain and suffering of others and even animals, bloodletting in the night. He had once sat in the barn torturing a wolf until it couldn't breathe anymore with his hand around its throat. The poor animal had stared at Jonathan with those mercilessly shimmering blue eyes until its brainwave activity and bodily functions had ceased.

"Can I do it here"?? Billy asked twisting the garrow or vein band around his left forearm.

"Not in my car". Jonathan ordered to pristine in taste to want or allow a junkies blood in his automobile. His worth, as he saw it was in plastic. Jonathan Dane was plastic, materialistic perfection had always been more his goal and style than all else unlike David who had in his life been all heart, champion to the bone.

David Dane had been raised to believe that Jonathan Dane was upstanding, a human being beyond reproach, but underneath a dark veil, Jonathan had been a completely different person whose character resembled a poisonous serpent with a wicked heart. He gave two shits about no one. Right and wrong did not exist. Jonathans existence was wrought with the worst and most vile evil that David Dane had ever seen. Even as a child, David had been locked in a room with hooks on the door and treated like a prisoner, a measure that would come back to distort his dreams later on in life.

"You never treated Andrew the way you treated me". David had once hollered at his Father during a blow up.

"Andrew didn't have the same problems that you did". Jonathan had scolded in a shrill, horrible tone.

In truth, it was David Dane who had been a whipping boy for his Fathers personal issues, a disgraced hero who went on to set the world on fire with his books all the while proudly baring the Canadian flag as the representative of the nation in his Family. David had reached feats that no one in his Family ever had or ever would and now CANADA was cheering for him.

As well, to his credit (Danes Uncle), Tom Wallace had proudly represented THE CANADIAN ARMED FORCES in HIGH MILITARY COMMAND thus giving him, by distinction the role of CANADIAN HERO. He had served as a Body Guard for many a dignitary and been involved in Covert Operations. Some mentionable names that Thomas had served as a Body Guard for were Pierre Elliott Trudeau, Prince Charles and Lady Diana, and as a cadet he had been awarded a medal by John F Kennedy. Dane had seen photos of the latter.

Danes Mother had represented Canada as a Figure Skating Coach for Special Olympics and was Canadian Alumni leading many of her athletes to gold medallions including one particular star nick named "Spit Fire". She had also at some point been nominated Coach Of The Year by Special Olympics Canada.

As a man Tom Wallace had been David Danes hero, many times, treating him like a best friend rather than a nephew. He had been a good man before his sad and untimely death a number of years ago due to organ failure. David Dane had cried a river of tears over his favorite Uncles passing, and no matter what would always hold a special place for him in his heart. Dane had many fond memories of he and Thomas driving through the darkness to Bear River late at night listening to Fleetwood Mac and The Pet Shop Boys. Thomas may not have been perfect, but his heart was always where it should have been, and above all else, he had honor, he also had so many medals and citations that Dane had at one time believed they may one day weigh him down.

One humorous story involving Thomas was when Dane had told his Uncle and a third party that during a court proceeding that he

(Dane) had told the judge that he was being insubordinate. Thomas had grinned broadly amidst an ironic nod and remarked to the third party- "Ye know that David had da nerve to tell the judge that he was being insubordinate" … … … … Thomas's reaction had nearly brought tears of laughter to Danes eyes. He was a good Uncle, the best, and Dane had loved him.

Tom Wallace had also served his country as the head of The Military Police where he had run Prisons and interrogated detainees from foreign countries who had been accused of Terrorism. Another of Thomas's accolades was that he had been a Terror Analyst for The entire Middle East.

One time after several hours of drinking, Thomas, inebriated and glassy eyed, had told Dane that he had fought in Vietnam. When Dane had reminded Thomas that Canada hadn't been in Vietnam and asked him who he had been representing, Thomas had replied-"Oh, myself son, myself". And after going further with it Thomas had characterized himself as "Da (Thomas slang for THE) one man assault unit. 2000 Soldiers a day, Fuck Rambo, Tom Wallace". The High Ranking Military Specialist boasted. Both he and Dane had laughed hysterically when Thomas had sobered up.

"Um, dis is yours"?? Ray asked of the pistol that sat atop Kate Shamrocks mantel. It was holstered, shiny polished black with a loaded clip chamber. "That's mine". The Irish Kick Boxing Titlist answered moving around the couch to where Wesley Snipes would be under study was standing.

"It's loaded because you are afraid, or because your Uncle taught you to leave it that way"?? The Sweet, Sweet, Black Man asked removing the gun from its holster.

"Both, I know that whoever killed Uncle Von may still be out there. Maybe I'm on their shit list". Kate said turning on the TV and pressing mute. Just then there was a sympathetic moan from the other side of the room. "Oh, you're such an angel". Kate said raising herself from the couch to go and greet WARRIOR who had just entered the room, chain jangling.

"Hi". She said kissing and cuddling the beautiful K-9.

WARRIOR was making adorable moaning sounds now as he closed his inquisitive brown eyes and enjoyed the attention he was getting. He had spent most of the evening sound asleep on the Queen sized bed with the canopy that Kate had bought for him curled up like a baby.

"Aww ... ... you're such a teddy bear". Kate commented.

"He, hee". Ray chuckled charmingly. "I think he likes having you pet him". The Ghana native remarked.

"Yeah, I think so to". She said.

It was then that the phone rang with her Mother on the other end. "Hey, how's Dad"?? Kate immediately asked. Her Father had been an emotional basket case lately and she knew it.

"He's alright I guess. I gave him a back and foot massage earlier so that relaxed him a bit".

"Can I talk to him?? Does he wanna talk to me"?? Kate asked shouldering her cell phone as she reached for WARRIORS leash that sat atop the refrigerator.

"I'm sure that he wants to talk to you but he's not here". Leilani informed her. "He just went back to the office to pick up some papers".

"Thanks Mom. I'll call him on his cell".

Andrew Dane stepped out of his Mercedes into the quiet night in a neighbourhood known all too well for its sinister addictions. He had parked close to Ontario and St. Alexandre De Seve and was now walking back toward a popular eating spot that he had recently grown fond of.

"Hello". He answered raising his cell phone to his right ear to hear Kates voice at the other end. "I'm on Ontario and Plesei right now he commented, shaking his gold watch into view. "If you wanna meet me here in twenty we can have dinner together". He offered. It had taken him about half an hour to get over here in heavy traffic but given the later time he believed Kate could make it in twenty.

"Okay, I'll see you soon". She said hanging up.

These were David Danes streets, he had made them world famous, but was no longer around to enjoy them. Just a short time ago they had lowered his Brothers casket into the earth and shovelled dirt on top of it before a crowd of on lookers. The image made him sick.

"Hey, you got any rolling paper"?? A dread with long hair and roller blades on asked. He looked thirtyish, unshaven and badly in need of a shower. "So, what up"?? He persisted glaring at the wealthy, sophisticated Andrew Dane.

"Nope, left mine at the office". Andrew responded, his expression unflinching. "I smoke up between representations". He said.

"Man, you like ... ... you must be kidding"?? The dread went on skating slightly backward on his wheels, his skin was tarnished with bruises. Andrew took them for being injection sights. He wasn't just a pot smoker the lawyer had discerned, he was also likely a Heroin addict.

"Uh-huh, i'm kidding". Andrew agreed walking on.

A few feet away Andrew saw a familiar looking face coming toward him. "Oh Andrew". Marcel began. "It is very bad what has happened to Von". The Frenchman said genuinely. "I have been at his Funeral. It was very sad". He said, his head dropping chin into chest.

"Thank you. I saw you there". The classy Andrew Dane said.

"Do The Police know who has done it"?? The Ontario Street HALL OF FAMER asked in a solemn voice.

"No, they have no leads. Hey, did my Brother ever mention anyone named Dee to you""??

Marcel paused for a moment seemingly in thought. The name rang the faintest of bells somewhere in his head. "It sounds familiar, but it is far away for me. I don't know where it has gone". He said. "If I think of it, I will tell you".

Andrew thought this an interesting revelation. If Marcel knew who this guy was it could help them out. "Here's my number at home and at work". Andrew said scribbling his digits on a scrap of paper and giving it to the Frenchman. "Anytime". Andrew said. "Would you like to join Kate and I for dinner, she should be here in about ten minutes".

"Oh, oui. I don't mind". Marcel said with his hands clasped behind his back soldier style. "It has make a long time that I haven't eaten in a restaurant".

"There's Kate". Andrew said noticing Kates sports car across the street.

MARCEL-I wanna take this time to address you old friend. I know that over time you and I have had our differences and that I've done some things to make you mad, I also want you to know that no matter what the shape of things, in the end, we're brothers in arms. It doesn't take a genius or a scientist with a degree to figure out that neither of us had it easy in our respective or mutual situations. We had to lose so we could win. I'll never forget our many funny conversations over the phone or in person when Monica was still alive and our mutual interests were hold up where they were. I also still remember your letter to a certain someone, and that one particular line-"You were cheating on me and playing those whore games". I recall telling you at the time that I couldn't believe what you had wrote and you said "Well, I have said it". I remember laughing until my heart almost stopped. Nonetheless, despite the doors, road blocks and long and winding roads, you are my friend forever.

Regards,

Von

CHAPTER II

"I think you need to find out what our pawn is doing outside of spending our money". The tall man, about six, six with the beard and the Armani suit said resting his gun on the table top. The room was quiet, empty of sound except for the bubbling of the aquarium that sat at an extreme edge of the shadowy rental space.

"I think he's a psychopath". The elder of the two men commented as the bearded assassin turned to glance at him over his right shoulder. "We should get rid of him, his presence in this matter makes me uncomfortable as it is, and over what"??

"If we get rid of him then we won't have any eyes or ears inside and we don't know what was said before hand or what information that bitch leaked". The bearded man said pouring himself a glass of Rum. It was windy outside, and the windows around them rattled and chattered. "I don't want to stay in Montreal any longer than I have to". He continued.

"We'll stay for as long as we need to". The elder of the two stated unbuttoning his blazer. "And all this because one woman opened the wrong door. "We never found the footage that she shot with her phone. She was holding up a phone on the monitor".

"Isn't that the whole problem"?? The bearded man asked rhetorically as his right hand sunk into the pocket of his dress pants. "It was that otherwise we wouldn't have had to have him kill her".

"All we have is his name. She was texting him before hand, and now he's dead. That was expert marksmanship". The bearded man remarked with a grin. "And a Canadian National Hero at that. I'll bet he never suspected a thing, not until he became an unwitting cupid".

"I think that he thought that she was dead up until that point". The elder of the two remarked gazing out the window toward Old Montreals Board Walk. It was an expensive accommodation, about five thousand per month but easily affordable to them. "First one then the other. He has bad luck. I guess she trusted him". The elder said splashing cologne on his pasty cheeks. "Where is she now he asked"??

The bearded man was shaking his head as he tossed back the ice in his tumbler. "I don't know. What did they do with her"?? He asked disinterestedly.

"Probably put her on ice somewhere. She could have been shipped back tax to The Netherlands for all I know".

"Bring the car around. I want to sleep". The elder said.

Kate Shamrock took a seat behind the banquet tables that had been set up on the beach as part of the presser for her next fight. It was hotter than Hell even below the umbrellas and cabanas that were set up all around them. "If I had known you were gonna bring your body guard then I would've brought mine". Shamrock commented affably as she stared across the table at her upcoming opponent.

"He's not here"?? Jill Walker teased.

"No, actually he's home taking his afternoon nap, he has to go to the vet later on, but I'll tell him that you're asking for him".

Jill nodded with humoured interest, she had flown in from Buffalo last night and was still slightly jet lagged. "Does your Body Guard have a name"?? Jill inquired.

"Warrior". Kate responded smoothly. "Believe me, he's a badass". She said with a tempered seriousness, giving him his due respect before breaking into a light smile.

Somewhere in the sky above them a small charter plane whirred before shifting course and heading east.

"Warrior, like his owner. I'm going to beat you on the twenty fifth and take your title". Jill assured the celebrated womens champion and pride of the Irish.

"I'll be bringing WARRIOR with me on the twenty fifth". Kate remarked to a round of chuckles. Jill was chuckling along with them. "You're going to need him". She said.

"Why, is he going to help you"?? Kate asked leaning forward to gaze at Jills six foot five protector who was standing in the sun wearing an ear piece and sun glasses.

"Nope, just me giving you the beating of your life".

"Your optimistic, it's not going to be that easy, I'm going to be in and out, just another day at the office. No hard feelings". Shamrock promised, lacing her response with her trademark savvy and finesse.

"We'll see". Jill said crossing one leg over the other underneath the table.

"Does anyone have any questions"?? Kate asked the barrage of media personnel who sat in sand rooted chairs before them.

"Kate, what do you think happened to Von "The Icon"?? A short stubby looking reporter asked.

"I think he's in Heaven". The Irish titlist replied with a strong trace of emotion in her voice. The issue was still sensitive, tears welling up in her pretty eyes.

Jill glanced sympathetically in her opponents direction. She had known Kate for a long time and had great respect for her, the two had trained in the same facility for a number of months when Kate was in The States, and during that time, Von had made several visits. He was a class act, hero to the bone. Many times he had overseen Kates training giving advice and pointers here and there, his death was a tragedy and she hoped his killer hanged.

"Why don't you find a different question to ask"?? Donovan O' Riley shouted from the back of the crowd. "I'm sorry me Gate. I would've been here earlier but me car had an oil leak". The Irishman stated as he made his way to the table.

"Hey ". Kate greeted as her trainer took a seat next to her. Donovan was as always dressed to the nines in apparel that reflected his nationality complete with a tammy cap and silk vest that read-LUCK OF THE IRISH on the back in shamrock green.

"Kate, is there any chance of you and Ronda Rousey ever stepping into the ring together"?? Another journalist inquired.

"I don't know". Kate said sporting a moderate smile, she had many times dreamt of fighting the legendary Rousey who was in many ways a superstar.

"Jill, how many rounds do you predict before a knockout over Kate"?? A tall good looking reporter questioned as Kate glanced over at her opponent with a smirk on her lips.

"I don't know, Kate will be tough to beat". Jill responded glancing back at Shamrock respectfully.

"Love you D". Kate said whispering in her trainers ear.

Just as the words were out of her mouth a series of three gun shots rang out across the beach two out of three of them hitting their marks as everyone scrambled to get out of the way.

"DONOVAN"!!! Kate screeched as her mentor crumpled to the ground in a heap. There was blood leaking from his nose and his mouth. He had been shot.

Jills body guard had lunged for her, but had instead missed his mark, and fell into the steps at the side of the rise where the table had been positioned. There was blood on his knuckles, but it was not his own, it belonged to Jill who lay dead a few feet away from him. He had listened to her final gasps as the air left her body for the last time. Donovan O' Riley was dead also after receiving a bullet to the neck. He had died in Kates arms.

"DONOVAN"!!! Kate cried aloud.

There was blood in the sand and in her hair. "OH GOD, OH GOD"!!! Shamrock sobbed as tears streaked her pretty cheeks.

The Shadow, thought of the final time that he had seen Von" The Icon "alive, the two had been in the park on Wolf and Mont Calm after having not seen each other in years. It was also the first time that Mathieu had ever met WARRIOR. There was an intense history between the two men who had for the longest time been rivals over Lilly Chicoines heart, but despite their hostilities, the two former sworn enemies had managed to come out the other end of the tunnel as friends.

Now, on this wet afternoon, the shadow stood below the overhang of a local Ontario Street Pub with a blue tooth positioned behind his ear. "Give me a call when you get here". The Shadow said to the person that he was speaking to, if it was too late he would leave and see the person on the other end of the line another time. He had made enough for one day, there had been a steady stream of calls for most of the morning but they seemed to taper off at lunch time. The Shadow walked away from where he had been standing, he wore bleached white runners below a black T-Shirt and beige shorts, as always the consummate fashion plate. The Shadow had not gone a day in his life without style as a trademark, always pimped up, never off it.

"Fuck, I wanna get high". The shadow told no one as the late afternoon current sailed around him, doing laps. The Quebec born French Canadian had been doing SMACK since trying it at a basement house party at the age of fourteen. He also did Coke, now he was forty years old and still trying to support his habit despite the perils of his predicament that of which included long stretches in prison, therapies, and doing whatever he had to do to get money. This was the road that Heroin addiction had paved for him, in that way, his story was a tragedy.

"You got anything for me"?? A pretty blond with a nose ring asked appearing from the shadows of an alley way".

"I'm not holding right now. I'm dry". The shadow said being honest with her, at least to the degree that he didn't have the product on him that she was looking for, of that, he had run out about an hour ago and was waiting for someone to come and stock him up tonight.

"Fuck, do you know who has any cause I need my shit". The blond said rubbing the ends of her nostrils with the knuckle of her first finger. She looked tired, eyes glassed over and fevered with her joans, sparkling, it had taken her out of work, out of home, and put her on the street.

"Call Manic, maybe he has something on him, I don't know. I was waiting for someone but I have to leave". The shadow said pocketing his ear piece. He was sick on the shit, bad enough, and he was on the outs with his Family, that was the nature of this thing, after a while short or long term, everybody got fed up. It wasn't as if he never tried, he had, but whatever the case the money and the green eyed monster had come calling on him. In the beginning, back when he'd first been stupid there had been a choice, a door, and he had walked through it eyes half open, now, there were the consequences. It was hard for The Shadow to believe that Lilly had ended up in the ground before him and even harder to believe that it had been Von who had come calling on him to tell him that she was dead, incredible, and on Facebook no less.

"You're here". The shadow said as his client finally showed up. He was tall with dark hair and a pinch, greasy, unwashed with a bad case of- I just woke up and I've got the shakes all over him.

"How many do you need"?? The shadow asked.

"Half, twenty's all I have". The man said.

"I'm gonna front you a point and you can pay me the other ten bucks later". The shadow said sympathetic from his own experiences, half wasn't gonna do shit, it would take at least a point before the Smack would work its magic, warm and fuzzy, best feeling in the world.

"Thanks bro, I'll have your ten in a few hours". The Doper promised.

"It's okay, I'm leaving, you can bring it to me tomorrow". The shadow said vanishing into the backseat of a cab.

When Kate awoke from her shock induced fainting spell she was face down in the sand and there were blood spatters all over her business suit, from head to toe. "DONOVAN"!!! She immediately yelped like a wounded animal.

"Wake". A voice from darkness came, only she was awake, and the sound of screaming and the distant surf were in her ears, thundering, hissing, droning, like an air craft engine flying to low, it was all around her now. Donovan was dead and she knew it, her unconscious mind longed for the comfort of her Uncle Von who always protected her, but now he was a part of a double nightmare. These people, these men, whoever wanted blood, wanted death, only for a reason that she did not know. There were scales of pain in her mind, rising, falling, doing laps, making everything a double haze.

"I can't see". Someone yelled, and then there was pandemonium, everyone running, together, separate apart.

"Jill's DEAD"!!! Her body guard who had failed yelled and somewhere inside he was drowning, no mercy and palpable, disconnected anguish, not fully tied in yet, but it soon would be. Kate wanted to make them pay for Jills death to, and by God no matter what they would.

"Can you hear my voice"?? A giant asked from above her. It was Dee, hand extended.

"Stop them. Where's your gun?? Do you have a gun"?? Kate asked not fully certain of what she was saying and then it seemed as if her soul was turned inside out as she rolled over and saw Donovans dead face staring wide eyed back at her, gone, never another kind word or a hug. Maybe it was all just a blood soaked nightmare and she would soon wake up in her bed but no such luck, realities agenda was different, evil, unforgiving.

There would if ever she could facilitate it be retribution of the most violent kind.

"Hold onto my neck". Dee said lifting Kate into his arms.

She was being carried away from the scene now by this goliath and out of the corner of her right eye, just past the retina she spotted Jills bloody corpse pushed haphazardly into the sand.

"Oh my God". She managed unearthing her voice from whatever realm … … … … …

"Did anyone spot the gunman"?? A shaggy looking journalist asked in a voice that sounded far off, distant, as if he were speaking through a tunnel.

"This is his I think". A man yelled sporting a toque hat at the end of his hand. He was standing above the make shift beach on the board walk, far above the sand dunes. The toque was more like a mask with the eyes cut out of it, chilling just to look at. There were two dead, no more life ever again and now Kate was asleep somewhere past the surf, on a tropical island, inset from a series of palm trees that were rooted out of the earth at different angles that bordered shadowy beaches.

"I'm over here, down here". A voice said, whose voice it was she didn't know. "I'm The Harbour Master". The voice said, deep, gravelly, seductive, and monotone all at the same time. "I'm the one who watches you, in sleep. I saw who killed your friends. His name … … … … … … … … Cloudless sky overhead again. "His name, is SANCTUARY" … … …

When Kate came to again she was flanked by six Police Officers who were standing above her looking down, watching, taking stock of the doctors actions. There was bright white light in her eyes now. They, someone, was examining her. "She's suffering from shock, it's a bad case but she'll be alright" Ryder said. He was the attending physician.

"Water". Kate mumbled. "I want water". And then somewhere Lilly was behind her eyes talking to her Uncle Von, it was like a playback from something that took place back in the days on Ontario Street, only this time silence, muted voices and Lilly doing her makeup in the field on De Lormier while her Uncle held a compact for her to see herself in. All of a sudden Lilly glanced over as if she could see the future and then the middle of night vision ended.

Monica-I want to break in here again to tell you that I hope you're enjoying NIGHTS END-URBAN RAIN III as it's brought to you. I hope that you're sitting up in Heaven at a Chapters or a Coles reading this. My God Monica, I miss our days and nights together so badly that I long only to have them back and for nothing else. I have never longed for, or missed another soul on this earth the way I do you. You were absolutely the love of my life, and the one flame inside of my heart that nothing will ever extinguish. I've never known another whose bravery was as great as yours. You're to be commended for that. I'm in love with you, now, forever, and beyond deaths door, eternally. My number one Bunny.

Love always,

Von

"Then I wanna know why nothing's being done about this"?? Andrew Dane hollered in the direction of the chief of Police who stood only feet away below a bright light that was set against a dim, rainy backdrop.

"Listen, Mr. Dane, we're doing everything we can but Ottawa Carleton has the collar on this case. We haven't developed a joint task force in this matter yet. We don't even have proof that whoever did this had anything to do with your Brothers assassination. Listen, we're doing everything we can". The Chief said tempering his remarks to sound more personal at the end.

"Do you know where they took my Daughter"?? Andrew asked, his cheeks aflame with rage.

"I believe that she was taken to The Montreal General per her own request".

"Sonovabitch". Andrew said underneath his breath as he shed his blazer and headed for the parking lot that stood just outside the front doors below the POLICE marquee. It was not that Andrew didn't believe that The Police were doing all that they could, it was, moreover that he thought that Montreal Regional should've been involved in the Police investigation surrounding his Brothers death from the beginning. Now, because of their fucking negligence, Donovan O' Riley was lying on a morgue slab, another woman had been killed and his own Daughter had very nearly ended up topping the list at number one, triple header.

"Your world is too dangerous". He reminisced saying to his Brother behind his eyes. They had been sitting in a hologram bar down in Florida just over a year before his demise. Kate had been there too, sipping a Margarita through a straw. "You and Lilly, do you have any fucking idea how many times the two of you could've been killed"?? He had asked, or in his Brothers words, demanded.

"No one asks for the hand they're dealt". He had responded never at a loss for words.

"Right, but you weren't dealt that hand, you came from a good home". Andrew had lamented never stepping over a vowel.

"This is your dime Drew. I had problems growing up and there was never peace in that house".

"Listen, you pulled some shit in that house".

"If I had a dime for every opinion I had to listen to I'd be as rich as you are. I'm not an instigator. Unfortunately our household growing up was a mixture of extremely diverse backgrounds and different personalities. It never fucking worked, never will". Dane retorted in the face of the wealthy barrister. "God forbid they ever make you a judge Andrew, ninety percent of the country will either be in jail or under house arrest, you'd probably be a bastard and put me under house arrest, in Mum and Dads house". Von remarked with a sly wit.

"Goodnight". Andrew said standing up and leaving the table.

Ray stepped out of a cavernous restaurant below the heat of old Montreals hot sun still oblivious to the events of the previous day, he had not watched TV nor listened to the radio, if he had, then he surely would have heard about the shooting, as he passed a pedestrian on the sidewalk he noticed the headline on the cover of the newspaper that was discarded on a table top- TWO DEAD IN ATTEMPT ON FEMALE KICK BOXING SENSATIONS LIFE.

"Oh shit". Ray said seriously followed by a slight moan as he lifted the paper into view. Kates photo was below the headline. "Oh Jesus Christ". He said reading the story that followed. "I have to call someone right away". He thought aloud.

"Yeah, I'm alright". Shamrock said smoothly sitting upright in her hospital bed. She had been in the hospital all night watching her Father sleep in a chair. "It's Donovan and Jill ... ..." She attempted breaking into a cry with her fingers pushed into her lower lip. "Those shots were meant for me. I should've died on that beach".

"Shhh ... ... hey". Andrew Dane comforted sitting forward. Leilani was also present in the room.

"No one, least of all you, meant for this to happen. This is evil honey, pure and simple. Maybe it had something to do with Von and maybe it didn't but either way The Police will find out". Leilani said length kissing her Daughter on the forehead.

"I want blood". Kate said straightening her voice.

"I came as soon as I heard". Ray said storming into the room about three minutes later. "I wasn't far away".

"Hey Ray". Kate greeted now standing upright on the floor with shadows from the blinds washing across her and invading her eyes that were sparkling with tears. In her head she saw her Uncle Von standing on the pier during their trip to Orlando, he was wearing a turquoise T-shirt over a pair of blue jeans above black sandals. "You pulled an all nighter". She had said approaching him in the hue of the late afternoon sun, somewhere droning from an airplane engine.

"I couldn't sleep, so I just kept walking around". He said. "I couldn't stop thinking about Lilly, about the fact that she'll never get to see all of this beauty". Her Uncle said with tears shimmering above a darkening sand. "I miss her more with every single day that goes by".

"I know". Kate had responded.

"You eat yet"?? Her Uncle asked putting his arm around her shoulders as she leaned into his chest.

"Nope, not yet". She answered arriving back in her hospital room face to face with her Uncles former flat mate.

"You were thinking about Mr. Magnum". The sweet, sweet, black man said removing his thin coat and hanging it over the edge of the bed rails.

"How did you know"?? Shamrock asked standing between her Father and Ray. "Because I know people. I can tell things just by reading your face".

"That sounds like something that Uncle Von would say. He had a special talent for that".

"Um yup!!! Mr. Magnum was good at reading people". Ray explained.

Just then Andrew Danes phone lit up. "Hello". He said answering the familiar tune. "Yes, yes, I'm his Brother". The Barrister said.

"My name is Brandy" The woman on the other end said moving around uncomfortably. "I have to talk to you". She said nervously as she kept vigilant over her Gothic Clothing Line Boutique with the high sales counter and low drop off.

"I'll be there in twenty minutes". Andrew agreed flipping his phone shut.

When Andrew Dane arrived at Brandys place of business he found the sexy curvaceous French Canadian raven haired Princess standing in the threshold of the doorway, she was wearing a denim jean jacket over blue jeans with rips purposely cut into them above high heeled pumps. He thought that she had a look that implied both style and seduction. She wouldn't be without attention he immediately registered.

"I found this in my mailbox". She said handing Andrew an envelope.

"What's in it"?? The Barrister asked, curious.

"It says it's from someone who saw your Brother die". She said. "I thought about taking it to The Police but I thought I'd let you read it first. There's no post mark". She continued as Andrew unfolded the lip of the envelope and began to examine its contents. The letter read as follows.

You don't know me but I knew your Brother. I was following him on the night he died. The people that your Brother was involved with are extremely dangerous. Killers all around you. Your Family may be targeted. Your Brother had information as well as other items that got him killed. He was a good man. You are in grave danger. Please take all precautions necessary to ensure the safety of your Family. Please heed this warning.

Take Care
God Bless
At the end of the letter Andrew looked up at Brandy. There was both fear and anxiety on his face.

"You missed your fucking target". The older man with the accent said on the other end of the phone. "His niece is still alive and we don't know what she knows. I trusted you with this and you failed for a second time. I wouldn't tolerate you if ... ...

The shadow on the other end, who had been listening moved to the door. There was crackling and static on the line.

"I want the entire Family dead next time. We've already searched both houses for safes. There are none. You need to silence the Danes forever.

I don't care what you have to do, the woman, her Father, and the model have to go".

The shadow on the other end was listening, its lips close to the phone. The shadow was wearing black leather driving gloves although the temperature did not call for it.

"Andrew Dane and his wife have a joint safety deposit in their name. There's going to be an emergency power down at their bank tomorrow and if there's anything in there our person will locate it. You have to do your job. If there are any more failures we'll no longer require your employment and you know what that means". The ominous foreigner warned turning his phone off.

Ray swung his car into the parking lot below Kate Shamrocks condo, he had been asked to go feed WARRIOR and that's what he intended to do. Once inside the apartment Ray was greeted by an enthusiastic WARRIOR who was wagging his tail frantically. "It is good to see you. I am going to get some food for you because I know you are hungry. Mr. Magnum would want me to tell you that he loves you". Ray said crossing the room to where the Hypoallergenic Dog Food was stored, but when he opened the door to the extended walk in closet he was greeted with a heavy blow to the skull.

Above him a tall figure stood looming like an evil spectre, it was Dee wearing a mask and gloves. Immediately, he searched Rays pockets but found only his wallet and a set of car keys with a pair of dog tags attached to them. "Fuck". He quietly lamented as WARRIOR who had been properly introduced to him as a friend wined and cocked his head to one side as if to ask for an explanation for what he was witnessing. "Good boy". Dee said standing up and walking out the door.

The person who had been on the phone with the foreigner moved across the room that they had not left all day or for days, it was hot outside, but the room boasted no AC making the acrid smell of sweat that hung in the air pungent.

The person would be here soon, the contact, and what was needed would be dropped off. It took a certain mind set, a certain discipline to do what needed to be done here, you didn't get it from a shoe box. This was about conviction, about making things what they should be forever, against those who needed to be silenced. This was justification in red, it was in the first place theirs to begin with.

"I'm willing to die". The shadow said. "I'm willing to die for what's mine". It said moving into the dimly lit bathroom to take stock of themselves in the mirror, smouldering eyes, radiant purpose, and a will to kill those who they felt had opposed them. "I'm willing to die". The shadow repeated and then began to laugh maniacally. "MOTHERFUCKER"!!! The shadow said before shattering the mirror with it's fist.

Blood and glass on the bath tubs forecourt.

Soon the shadow rested itself into a fetal position on the ground and closed its eyes. There was fluid everywhere, crimson and sparkling, shimmering, shining glass.

In half an hour a tall well groomed man was at the door wearing a grey Armani suit and sun glasses. He spoke with an accent as he explained what needed to be done. He was himself a killer, an assassin by trade although this way would be easier, and there was more to speak to here besides business, an agenda farther serving, and he was willing to sacrifice for his cause.

"Here, this is what you'll need". The man said preparing the clip on a fire arm for the shadow who lay across from him on the floor. "If the jobs not done right this time I think you know what'll happen". The assassin warned staring at the shadows back.

"Yeah, alright". The one who was laying down responded.

"I'll leave this here". The killer said leaving the gun on a table. "Get cleaned up. Go do what you have to do. I'll be back in the morning". He said.

Kate Shamrock loaded her bag into the trunk of her Fathers car and walked toward the passenger door. It was late, close to one a.m., as she exited the reflective black doors below the surveillance cameras that lead onto the parking lot that existed as two stories. As she looked to her far left she saw a shadow standing idol, as if watching her.

"Dad". Kate exclaimed as she attempted to bring the spectre to her Fathers attention, but when he looked, the figure was gone as if it had evaporated back into the night from which it came. "Did you see that"?? Kate asked as her Father peered over the roof of his expensive automobile.

"No, what"?? He quickly responded.

"There was somebody standing over there. It looked like they were wearing a ski mask with the eyes cut out of it". She said brushing the rim of the car roof with her forearm.

There was desolate silence in the parking lot as if they were suspended inside of a dream, the fantastic and the surreal. Kate thought eerily imagining Ontario Streets darkened alleyways and alcoves somehow years before she had seen them. A different time, and the sandman singing a little tune. Somehow the night had lived to rise up on her, to leave her without the protection or comfort of her Uncle Von. This entire ordeal was a nightmare.

The shadow that had been on the phone with the foreigner moved in circular fashion before sitting down in a chair by the wall. Madness had come to live in a brain that had been tormented, whistled about, and had leaves blown across its graters for years, and in time, had turned to pure insanity. Now there would be retribution of the most evil and sinister kind, a betrayal so monumental that the world, and the world that had come to know the shadow by another name would not believe it. There was darkness now in the cathedrals of this individuals brain, doors with tape running across them, sealed off. Alone, the shadow thought of the one thing that it believed mattered most, to destroy its enemies, all of them. Once this person had believed in kind righteous things, things that bore no resemblance to the wicked person that the shadow from Hell had become, this demonic presence that once knew love and how to show it, had lost all sense of compassion and decency.

There was a clicking sound outside the door causing the shadow to raise from its position and shift directions in the room. Was it one of them, or their own they?? A THEY, A THEM, every paranoid schizophrenic had one, and the shadows case was no exception because the shadows mind believed it was being watched, seen from an invisible control room inside, darkened except for the eternally glowing monitors that watched, saw, and recorded everything simultaneously. There no longer, for the sake of reality existed any concept of right or wrong for the sake of unholy justification, there existed only a will to kill, to eliminate, too conquer the enemy.

"Hello". The shadow(Different Person than above) alone said but there was no one there, dead air and unholy silence. It was as if all of mankind had evaporated, dissipated bit by bit in the night, now there remained only wicked torment, and gun fire. It had been another time and another place that had born this mindset, it was a mindset with nothing left, its drapery masking an agenda of pure evil.

In the night the shadow had dreamt of a train station with a sloped floor where something terrible was supposed to happen, its certainty unknown. There were people there, strangers, and the train seemed to lead to nowhere, a far off with no given name. The images had been hypnotic, mesmerizing but without true reason or merit. Around here, in dreams, horror had a special and unique way of presenting itself, quiet, subdued, abandoned.

Alone, the shadow reached for the firearm and drew its barrel towards its own head squeezing the trigger to produce two hollow metallic clicks. No off switch, no ending, only darkness and the droning of the A.C. across the hall.

"Yeah, I'm bad. I do bad things". The shadow said. "I've lied, I've used people, I can't lie and say that I never used Lilly Chicoine. I should've left her there with Von but I didn't. I shouldn't have done that. Am I irredeemable? I guess that's your own opinion. I do whatever I have to do to get money for drugs. This is the sickness, the disease called addiction. I'm afraid that I've stained Lillys life with mine, and now, she's gone forever. I wanna say that I'm sorry but there's no taxi service to take me to Heaven.

If you knew everything, my whole story from A to Z then you might understand, then again, you might wanna see someone kill me".

"Did you do it on purpose"?? The pretty blond girl asked.

"What, make Lilly what she became?? Yeah, I did. I met her at a rave called Sona and I knew that there was potential there. I foresaw that if I could make her love me, if I could get her hooked on Smack that she would pay for everything. You can't imagine my shock when I saw her getting in and out of cars. Then on Halloween night 2000 I met Von and everything changed".

"Why"?? The blond asked.
"Because she became his girlfriend and I went to jail. Man, there were times when I thought that Von was gonna punch me right in the face but he never did, he has a heart, and I got to know him. Say, you got a cigarette"?? The shadow asked switching positions on the ledge where he sat. They were sitting on the front steps of a poorly maintained apartment complex behind Frontenac in the darkness and drizzle. The shadow had come here to cop dope, the girl just to listen, and because despite his past, she enjoyed his company.

"Here". She said passing him a fresh smoke.

"Thanks". He responded placing it between his lips and firing up hand over stick to protect the flame from the rain. It was coming down harder now, drizzle to downpour and he had no jacket. "I guess I can smoke this here. I'm starting to come down from my buzz".
Just then a tall junkie with a punk rocker Mohawk and trimmed sideburns walked into the buildings vestibule, obviously here for the same reason, fucked up, likely hadn't slept for a while. The shadow registered. His brow was twitching and he was dry sniffing. If he remembered right this guy had done speedball with him once, years ago.

"What's up bro"?? The shadow asked him.

"Nothing, I'm really fucked up. If I get a hold of a gun I'm gonna do an armed robbery". The dread said paid up, worked, and badly in need of quiet and sleep. Aggression was a side effect of way to much Cocaine and not enough sleep, it was also one of the first things that any hospital triage nurse would ask if you called in to a hospital cause you thought you'd done too much and were in need of medical attention. "Are you an aggressive person by nature"?? Because if you were then Coke would exacerbate your condition.

"I don't have a gun. That's not smart". The shadow warned. "I did a lot of pen time. You don't wanna go back there if you've been there before. Back in the early 2000's I had like fifty charges against me and they kept pulling out new ones every time I tried to walk out the door. They say I'm at high risk for offending again".

"Yeah". The Rocker responded, half in the bag. He knew that it was not polite to ask about some ones charges and that if the person really didn't like you then it was a shankable offence, you could get stabbed even though he didn't think the shadow would do that.

Jonathan Dane lifted the veil on what the plan was as he moved across the floor of his makeshift church wearing a black cloak over a grey suit. Cyril Mathews was also present seated next to a portable smoke machine that he had purchased from a movie crew many months ago. There was also money tied up in this ministry, tens, if not hundreds of thousands of dollars rested on the line if things didn't pan out. There had to be many donations, and there were, for their cause had many charitable members who sought to serve the same God that they did. There would be an ambush on Kate Shamrock, Andrew Dane, and Leilani in the dead of night where Kate would be the only extraction from the house. Following that she would be brought here, and changed forever. She would become like her Grand Father and his creatures, Jonathan wanted no part of her that wasn't corrupted remaining, her thoughts were to mirror his. Evil Angel. Mathews thought putting aside the long cigarette he had been smoking, dipping its ash into an ashtray.

Smoke rising into darkness.

At the house two of Jonathan Danes disciples climbed the balcony and began to stalk the inner perimeter of the condo each prepared with a hunting knife and grappling hooks. Inside, limitless darkness and abandoned alcoves. No security system had been tripped and no one had come running, there would be no exchange of gunfire, no lives sacrificed in the wake of their mission, although both Derek Muldiva and Billy Turner were prepared to die, Jonathan Dane was their master and they would do as he asked, no matter their own fate. They were here to extract Kathleen Dane Shamrock from the house and at the same time eliminate two obstacles, no matter how savagely.

"There's someone in there". Billy said pointing toward a second story door with three carpeted stairs leading up to it. "Go". He urged as Muldiva began his ascension toward the plush steps and kept habits of sleep, nestled away below the sheets, muted in darkness.

"SONOVABITCH"!!! Andrew Dane Hollered from behind as he swung a baseball bat at Billy Turner.

"DEREK"!!! Billy yelled as Muldiva was swinging around to respond to what he had just heard.

Now, there was the opening of a door as Kate Shamrock appeared out of nowhere skillfully dispatching Derek Muldiva with a standing side kick to the Adams Apple sending him over the railing at the top of the stairs, killing him.

Soon, two more figures appeared in the house as Leilani Dane exited her room with a glass object in her hand. She was screaming as her husband fist floored the first of the two. Shamrock was in form now, ready for a violent onslaught of whatever variety.

As Leilani attempted to negotiate the carpeted condo stairs she caught the blade of a knife in the rib cage causing her to crumple to the floor, wounded, but not dead.

Outside on the front lawn, below the terrace there was the squealing of tires and then several more of them appeared, only this time there was somebody standing in their path, it was the masked figure from the hospital parking lot Kate recognized even from her vantage point inside the house. He, whoever he was, was obviously here.

The masked figure who had been outside all night began to dispatch Jonathan Danes killers with expert precision using, hands, feet, and a black lead pipe.

Andrew Dane was tossing opponents one and then another head first into a plaster wall by his study before receiving a glancing blow to the head rendering him unconscious.

Shamrock was at the top of the stairs, hands and feet working, and she hadn't even broken a sweat. Whoever had trained these pieces of shit hadn't done a very good job, there wasn't one of them who had any technique.

The masked figure was inside now removing one threat after another. He was totally clad in black his identity concealed by a hood and ski mask.

"MOM"!!! Kate yelled finally noticing her Mother motionless on the floor far below her.

The figure eye balled Leilani concernedly but then continued to do battle with Jonathan Danes henchmen.

When there was no one left the shadowy hero eye balled Kate from the foot of the stairs holding his gaze for a moment, as if communicating with her mentally before turning away, exiting the house, and disappearing into the deep twilight of the eerily quiet nocturne.

When The Police arrived fifteen minutes later Andrew Dane was holding a cold compress against the back of his head as Leilani was carried off on a stretcher. Kate was there sitting on the stairs still suffering the effects of the shock. In moments she'd be on her feet and riding to the hospital with the woman who had given birth to her.

"So you don't recognize any of these guys"?? Officer Blane asked.

Andrew was shaking his head. "No". He answered honestly looking around at the heap of bodies that the masked figure had left behind.

"And you say that someone showed up out of nowhere to help you, and he did all of this"??

"That is exactly what I'm saying. Would you like me to spell it out for you"?? Andrew retorted, not in the mood for a line of questioning.

"What'd he look like"?? Blane asked, pen to pad.

"I have no idea, he was wearing a mask". Dane responded.

Kate was on her way out the door behind the EMT's now. "I'll see you at the hospital". She directed toward her Father who was sitting on the stairs.

"Okay". The Barrister said.

"You didn't see anything else? Did he speak"??

"Yeah, Oprah walked in and he did a ninety minute interview on the state of the economy".

Blane sighed, satisfied that Andrew was telling the truth. He didn't believe that someone of Andrew Danes caliber would lie under such circumstances anyway, and these were serious circumstances. There were nine dead bodies in this house.

"Can I go and see my wife now"??

"You're free to go. My partner will follow you to the hospital. He might wanna talk to you some more when you get there". Blane concluded flipping his pad shut.

"We're gonna need a statement from your Daughter too". Blane assured him.

"Only in my presence". Andrew Dane replied, and that was that.

"Your people failed". Cyril Mathews informed the cloaked figure who sat at the far end of the room below a large red oil painting of a strange looking creature. There was no sound from darkness, only the humming of the air conditioning system that was mounted in a far wall.

"Someone showed up. I mean who in the hell was it, a security person"?? Jonathan pondered amidst the scent of sulphur that was rising from the burnt out candles that had been placed around the deeply shadowed room.

The image of the room seemed somehow to burn into itself over and over again, hypnotically, like an image from night.

"You need to kill your son and his wife. They're what's keeping you from your Grand Daughter". Cyril lamented with a fused, ignitable passion.

"It's so strange, you strike at the throat of your enemies . . . .

Just then a figure appeared in the doorway.

"I called for you earlier". Cyril said to the individual who now stood in their wake. "Why can't you ever be here when you're needed? Our targets had an unexpected guest tonight, a man".

"Who was the guest"??

"You need to gain enough leeway to her to kill her Family". Cyril said walking across the floor with his hands clasped behind his back soldier style. "If we haven't paid you enough already then we will. I need you to do this job, and you have a personal stake in it so I don't know why it hasn't been accomplished before now".

Fire from below in a gust.

"You need to find it in yourself again, and I doubt they'll see you coming".

The other man on the third side of the room was laughing now, there was a scar running the length of his bitterly shaped face, twisting, and burrowing itself in just below the jaw line.

"When can I see her"?? The man who was wearing a three piece suit asked. "It'll be my pleasure. I'm not happy to hold anyone up but I'm going to ask you for more money". The face of evil and night itself said. "I can kill for you again, as bad as that might seem to certain people".

"Then we'll pay you what you need". Cyril Mathews guaranteed. "We'll pay you what you need. We're not going to short change our policy".

"You just make goddamn sure you do it right this time". Jonathan Dane said, no patience or joy for life, necessity first all else second.

"You made me, my sacrifices are for you". The man said.

"Wake". Someone said, and then the eyes, at least the eyes that were inside of Leilani Dane opened onto the freshly painted hospital room that she had been placed in, but something was wrong, something strange, and she felt as though she was paralyzed, unable to move or speak. "Hmm uh" … … … She managed but then the faces of Jonathan Danes men were all around her glaring at her as if a part of her was reliving the nightmare from earlier in the evening. Somehow Derek Muldiva was mounted on top of her wagging his tongue in her direction as Billy Turner and two others were wielding knives at her bedside.

"Mom, can you hear me"?? Kates voice echoed from another dimension, somewhere, someplace away from here, wherever here was. Now, she was caught in a fusion of dreams, a chain of cavernous nightmares that she seemed far too unlikely to awaken from. They were rising from all corners of the sterile room now beginning to form shapes and shadows on the walls and behind the curtains, becoming part of the flooring and even the tile, painted grey, watching, moaning, salivating at the mere idea of savagely torturing or raping her. This was the very definition of evil by its own genesis, and then there were burning candles atop an altar in a dark room and the focus of the nightmare shifted again to a cell with no doors or windows where she was chained fitfully to the wall with wrist bracelets. "HELP ME"!!! She finally managed before a section of the wall seemed to remove itself to reveal Jonathan Dane, her Father in law, trailed by three hooded druids carrying incense burners on chains that clasped at the top.

There were low voices and sounds that seemed to belong in death chambers from medieval times gone by a hundred centuries ago.

"ANDREW"!!! She finally hollered before tossing herself violently against the railing of her hospital bed as she finally joined the living world again, awake to a room full of rain shadows.

When Kate awoke she was in the front seat of some ones car being driven along a darkened stretch of road to a town simply known as NIGHTS END. "Can you hear ... ... She attempted below the veil of drugged consciousness, but the driver whose face she couldn't make out would not respond. All that she was able to discern from her vantage point was that the driver who minded the road was wearing a shadowy mask and a hood much like the person who had entered her Fathers house, filling her mind and her heart with a question that she could not answer.

This was a place, unknown, and particularly to her. Somewhere she saw a car burning along a stretch of highway that she somehow knew it was Lillys although Lillys car had never burned, then there was an epitaph on tomb stone that was rooted someplace in the earth-It's exact words spoke to Ontario Streets past-It said-BEWARE ALL YEE WHO ENTER HERE SHALL SUFFER ETERNAL DAMNATION, and indeed so many of The Ontario Street Originals had, now simply ghosts who wandered Ontario Streets Alleyways and alcoves long after sundown, in the quiet wee hours of the morning.

As they sped along the road the firemen fought to put out the flames that were shooting from the windows of Lillys Nissan Maxima, each one working feverishly to keep the blaze under control. There were tears welling up in Kates eyes now as she remembered the legendary urban angel that her Uncle had always loved unconditionally, if ever there was a woman who could do no wrong in a mans eyes then it was Lilly Chicoine in the eyes of her Street King Uncle, he had, had a love for her that nothing could ever have matched, not in a thousand milleniums, a love that he had died with under the cloak of an Ottawa night.

As they turned off of the main through fare to this place there seemed to be an acoustic sigh as the man put the car in neutral and let it roll past the big oak wood sign that read NIGHTS END in BOLD ITALLYCS. Kate did not know where she was or where she was going but only that bad things were going to happen here, horrible, terrible unspeakable things.

An hour later when she came to fully she was alone in the front seat of the car accompanied by no one. The Driver had absconded leaving no forwarding information. Now, she was here in this desolation all alone. Shamrock had never wished that WARRIOR was with her so badly in her life, and at some point, she sobbed fearfully and shouted his name but there was no response.

"Hello". Kate mumbled curled up in the fetal position close to the handle of the front seat passenger door. She wished for the man in the mask to return, but no such luck, he had vanished into the engulfing blackness of wherever this was. It was like a scene from a fever dream that you might have lying in a dark room on a mattress somewhere as reality and fantasy tried desperately to fuse itself back together again.

After another few minutes had elapsed it dawned on her that the radio might work or be able to give her some information, for although the man had absconded, he had left the engine idle.

"Come on dammit, work". The highly disciplined Shamrock fussed but there was no such luck, all that the radio produced was an ominous static with a touch of a frequency wine.

"I have to get out of here". She said opening the door and falling onto the ground outside the vehicle.

"C'mon work". Kate said trying to nurture the feeling in her legs into coming back. It was obvious that whatever she had been given hadn't worn off yet, still under the influence.

Soon she had passed out waking a second time to someone carrying her cradle style through the night that seemed to lead across a footbridge with a stream running below it, again she recognized the darkly clad figure to be the masked man from the house the other night.

"Who are you"?? She asked, but the man gave no response.

Further down the road Kate noticed what appeared to be a bunch of cultists performing a ceremony in blackest night, each one cloaked in a hood accompanied by a red silken scarf with symbols on it and someone was spreading what looked like ashes over the earth.

As they got closer the man in the mask put her down gently before engaging in hand to hand combat with each of the evil spectres rendering one after another of them unconscious or disabled in order to protect her, because in her current state, even the highly trained Kate "The Gate" Shamrock was to drugged to defend herself.

Soon, and not before long they were in a mall with heavily bleeding spotlights that cast lots of eerie shadows across the merchandise in the stores. It looked like a B RATED HORROR FLICK Kate registered, and again, however casually, the masked man was close to her side as if shopping like a regular mall patron in this carousel of the fantastic, this rock video turned inside out, a song, and a place, called NIGHTS END.

In a couple of hours she seemed to wake up again, this time back in the car. As she sat upright and stretched her arms Kate looked through the scratched windshield to see a small, sea side town with cabins row after row on gently sloped hilltops, each with a newly painted bright orange door and matching drapes. She neither recognized her surroundings nor believed that she had ever been to this quiet little sea side resort ever before.

"Where am I"?? She asked no one but the eerie desolation, for although it was warm and sunny here, there was something very disquieting, if not unnerving about this place, it made her feel queasy in presence alone, nerves, the kind that you felt while waiting for important blood test results or the indignation of a vaginal exam.

Where was the masked man, and what had made him decide to abscond again??

Was this reality or something that her unconscious mind had dreamt up??

"Fuck". She said realizing that she was buckled in and doing something release herself from the seatbelt at the same time. There was no one here, all alone. What the hell had happened to everybody and had anybody ever been here in the first place.

"Welcome to NIGHTS END". She said stepping out of the automobile and beginning to walk down the centre of main street that was occupied by absolutely no one, not a soul. Somewhere in her mind it had for a moment dawned on her that not only did she not have a clue where the fuck she was but it was also likely that no one else did either, and that included Andrew and Leilani Dane.

"I can't believe this". The beautiful Shamrock said looking around from one length of her vision to the other. One of the first things that Kate noticed was that the grass on the gentle slopes and front lawns of this shanty town was fresh however uncut as if no one had bothered to tend to its maintenance in a while.

Where the fuck was she and how exactly had she gotten here, also an interesting question. Who ran this place??

Just as that thought escaped her mind Kate noticed someone peeking out from behind the drapes of a nearby cabin. Short woman, plump. My God this place made her uneasy, almost sheepish, a state of mind that the fearless shamrock had seldom in her life ever experienced.

"They're going to kill you".

"What"?? Shamrock asked looking around for the source of the voice that seemed above her somewhere, as if spoken from the confines of a metal room.

Down two more streets and around a short corner Kate came to a small shop with tinted windows and a painted chariot shadowing the window.

"Hello". She shouted from the slight porch but no one answered her call.

Jesus, this place was surreal.

"I know you". A voice called from an alleyway between two cabins.

"Hello". Kate shouted a second time.

"I'm Natasha". The dirty blond said emerging from the early afternoon shadows of this place.

"Hi, I'm … … … … … … … … … …

"Kate Shamrock". The girl responded before Kate could.

"You know me"?? Shamrock asked prepared to raise hell if she had to.

"I know you". Natasha said through a French accent, although this town was hardly French. "We may only get ten or twelve channels in this place but we get the newspaper".

Kate was nodding and squinting in the silver glint from a car that sat by the curb. "I see". She said, a two word response that she had definitely inherited from her Father. "It's nice to meet you". Shamrock greeted smoothly, ambience of calm, she had enough confidence to over shadow the marines.

"Yeah, I knew your Uncle to". Natasha disclosed.

"You knew Uncle Von"?? Kate asked with a touch of defensive bewilderment in her voice. How the hell did this woman know her late Uncle, and who in Christs name was she??

"Yeah, we met in 2011". Natasha stated with a subtle smirk clearing somewhere in her expression.

"Really"?? Kate responded, waiting for a full on.

"On Ontario Street. Your Uncle was a big, big hero there". The girl said.

Shamrock wasn't getting a good read from this woman. "You're a friend of Uncle Vons"??

"The best". Natasha said leading Kate a short distance down the badly kept broken side walk of wherever the fuck they were. It somehow felt like there was a hand held camera following them, not quite reality.

"So, where exactly are we"?? Shamrock inquired already both leery and weary of her only company in this nightscape.

"Nights End". Natasha said almost dancing around Shamrock in a way that was mocking.

"Nights End, and that's off of what highway or stretch of road"?? Kate asked still unsure of just exactly what the fuck was really taking place here. Something was wrong.

"Oh, it's a little ways outside of some of the really big places in Canada".

This was definitely getting past the point of strange. Shamrock registered. This blond girl in the grey stretch dress with the stains on it was weird, that and she had an odour about her that wreaked of semen.

"Are you here for a fight or did you just happen down a rabbit hole"?? Natasha asked the prize fighter.

"Just passing through". Shamrock responded not knowing how else to answer, and she did not like this woman nor did she believe her to be a friend of her Uncles.

"I'll give yah ten bucks to suck it off for me". A stale smelling, foul old man with a horrific body odour asked Natasha from behind a cabin door. "C' mon Missy, we had a good time that night that you defecated on me remember"??

"Listen, I have to go". Shamrock said turning away from Natasha in utter disgust as Natasha egged the pervert on. "Okay, I'll let you eat my asshole to". Natasha promised chasing Shamrock down the sidewalk. "Leave me alone". Kate ordered. "I mean it". She said, the fighter coming out of her all at once. She wanted and would have nothing to do with this creature ... ... NOTHING!!!

As Kate put several blocks of distance between she and Natasha she noticed a busty, short haired blond standing by a tiny convenience shop with a leaky roof.

"Hi". Kate began in a winded voice. "And you are"?? She asked.

"Jersey". The sexy blond bomb shell who had once known Natasha but who would now have not a thing to do with her said. "Nice to meet you".

"I just met a really strange person, I'm sorry but I'm a little rattled". Kate said.

"There are a few of those around here. I'm sorry". The sexy voluptuous Jersey apologized. "Who did you meet"??

"I think she, and believe me I use the term loosely, called herself Natasha". Kate explained.

"We used to be best friends but then she did something that I can never, ever forgive to a special friend of mine".

"Who was the friend"??

"I'm not supposed to disclose that here". Jersey said dropping her smile and heading directly across the street to a waiting car. "I'm sorry, I have to go, nothing I can do about it".

"Wait, what do you mean here"?? Kate asked moving anxiously in Jerseys direction only to watch the car that she had disappeared into roll away.

Well, at least there are people here. Kate thought walking further along the sidewalk toward a series of vehicles that were headed down the street next to her.

Not supposed to disclose that here. What had she meant?? Kate pondered.

"I wish I had you all a-lone, just the, two of us". Kate sang, and then wondered where and how she had picked up those lyrics.

There was wavering static somewhere in her brain like radio interference … … … … "You've been shot in the head". A voice from nowhere came, it seemed to belong to nothing and no one.

"Hi Kathleen, do you know who I am"?? The old woman with the crooked teeth, out of date blouse, and brown checkered skirt asked.

"I'm sure I have no idea". Kate responded again shocked at the fact that there was someone here who knew who she was.

"My name is Myrtle. I knew your Uncle when he was in grade school". The old woman wearing the tinted reading glasses said.

"No, I don't think that could be possible".

"Oh, believe me I did". The wrinkled faced woman who looked like she ought to be riding a broom said.

Jesus, Season Of The Witch. Shamrock thought to herself. Who the hell was this old weirdo who wreaked of bug bomb??

"You need to run along, run along". The witch urged wickedly as Kate frowned and heeded her advice. What the hell was this place, and what were these people all about??

Down a rabbit hole. Kate thought to herself ironically, that was about the extent of it.

Suddenly, with almost no time passing it was night again as if the remaining daylight hours had been systematically removed without explanation.

"Scalpel" A voice echoed from somewhere yet nowhere.

In about fifteen minutes Kate came to a giant steel and metal structure that was sitting on a hilltop overlooking Nights end that resembled a warehouse or a storage facility for large vehicles. "What the hell"?? She asked only the night. "Christ this place is eerie". Shamrock commented.

"May I help you mam"?? A tall lanky gentlemen with bad breath and rotten teeth asked. His hand was on Kates shoulder.

"Who are you"??

"Most folks around here call me Deke but my real name's Derek". He said. "How come you're out here prowlin around where you don't belong"?? He asked accusingly.

"Oh, I was just looking for a place to use the rest room". Kate lied.

"Well, you aint gonna find nowhere like that around here". The hick said sternly.

"I'm sorry, I'll go someplace else then". Shamrock apologized. "What is this place exactly she asked".

"The warehouse"?? Deke went on. "That's a place that you never wanna end up no matter what you done nor to whom". He said. "Bad things happen to the best of us up there".

"Whadya mean bad things"?? Kate asked watching a car with a strange looking driver in it roll by.

"I can't tell yah nor more than that, they might be listenen or watchin us on one a them monitors". He said with anxiety beginning to rise in his voice. "It's time for me to go".

On his final words Kate watched Deke vanish into the deep twilight of the night as if he were being swallowed whole by it. The blackness had seemingly turned Deke into a vapor.

The darkness was somehow making everything appear that much more ominous and threatening then it had in the daylight.

Suddenly the focus changed like a scene from a movie and now Kate was in an eerie looking hospital room with glowing yellow pilot lights spilling in from the darkened corridor outside. The lights in her room were off.

"Where am I"?? Kate mumbled and sobbed at the same time, but no reply came. Out the window and across the way Kate could vaguely make out a murky looking orange sign that read-NIGHTS END MEMORIAL HOSPITAL.

"Why am I here"?? She sobbed turning her head to the left on the pillow.

"You were attacked tonight". A tall Doctor with sand coloured hair and a moustache said. He hadn't been standing there before, but now he was.

"I don't understand". Kate lamented, confused.

"Don't you remember"?? He asked in a strong but friendly voice. "You were babysitting and you had a run in with a man in a mask. Do you know a Jaime Trenton"?? The handsome Doctor asked as he fastened a blood pressure cuff to Kates bicep.

All of this reminded her of something, but she didn't know what, even the Doctor.

In seconds she could feel the pressure rising in her arm and in her head, everywhere, only now the Doctor who had been by her side, the one with the pock marked cheeks and the red shirt had completely vanished. She was again, all alone.

In a few moments there seemed to be a soundtrack or score in her head, in the whatever and wherever, it made her think of being forlorn, of abandoned desolation, or a traumatic childhood.

Had Jaime Trenton been the man in the car or had that been someone else?? The Doctor had said something about baby sitting and a man wearing a mask. No, it didn't seem that way. The man in the car had been her friend, not some evil stalker.

Now, she was more afraid then she had been before. Where was this stalker named Jaime now??

In seconds a light skinned nurse with a pretty face and wide eyes had come to join her.

"This will help to calm you down". The nurse said producing a syringe full of whatever.

"No, don't put me to sleep". Kate moaned painfully but the nurse administered whatever was in the needle anyway. "You get some rest". She urged.

Several hours later Kate woke up and threw the covers back certain that if she did not get the hell out of here that she would almost certainly die tonight. "Where are you"?? She asked, wondering if the man who had attacked her was still someway, somehow after her.

It was gloomy out in the corridor, and Kate had an I.V. strapped to her. There was also a bandage around her knee that had a massive blood stain on it. It was somehow a form of Déjà vu, as if she had either lived or seen all of this somewhere before.

Now she was outside in the corridor although she had no recollection of having made her way there whatsoever. The yellow pilot lights that glowed ominously throughout the hospital gave an evilish if not sinister back drop to the night inside around her.

"Help me". She begged as if someone or something was willing her to utter those words as she hobbled along on one foot switching to the other for only seconds at a time.

Someplace else in town, the masked man who had driven Kate to NIGHTS END was inexplicably riding shot gun with a familiar looking Sheriff in a Police Cruiser, ski mask and all, yet the Sheriff uttered not a word of exception to the man, his wardrobe nor his highly unusual presence in the car, it was just as if all of this was routine.

"You let him out". The Sheriff scolded to which the man in the mask shook his head, he had not let anyone out, this Sheriff was delusional.

"His own goddamn … … … … … …

Then there was an interruption on the radio stating that people were beginning to imitate characters from books and films and accept them as being real, they were even killing and mutilating each other over it.

The man in the mask looked in the Sheriffs direction now.

"There have been a series of homicides tonight at the hands of THE NIGHTS END KILLER also known to locals as Jaime Trenton". The Radio D.J.'s voice echoed ominously across the air waves out of tune.

Kate pulled herself along the corridor, hand dragging against the deep nocturnal shadows on the wall for support. It was as if this was something that she had seen somewhere else, somewhere in a movie, once again reflective of where she'd been or what she'd seen in her life that she could not place. Now here, in this place, there was no one to help her, even her masked saviour had absconded leaving her to fend for herself.

Suddenly her surroundings changed again and now she found herself wobbling down a long dark stretch of road towards a chain link fence and a trio of smoke stacks that reached far up into the night, orange in color with white bands.

"Where am I"?? She asked the rippling blanket of winds that sailed ominously around her. "Uncle Von"!!! She called out for no discernible reason, but there was no response, only darkness and the winds.

Somewhere in the distance Kate noticed a shadow moving in silhouette against the back drop of this dreamscape. It was Lilly dressed in a blue shirt and denim jeans, same as she had been wearing the night that the two had for one time and one time only locked eyes outside of The Domino, the same night that Lilly had confronted Eva.

"Lilly"!!! Kate called out trying to hobble toward the legend, but no such luck, the winds and the knee wound were holding her back, and Lilly was gone, once again a part of the night and this place wherever this place was that she had appeared from.

"Chicoine"!!! Kate yelled somehow trying to revive the image of her Uncles deceased love but there was no response from empty, desolate, forlorn darkness that seemed somehow to pulsate with smooth, rhythmic drumbeats that were all around her.

As Shamrock turned a corner she suddenly saw a man wearing a white mask stalking her with a butchers knife clenched in his fist, he bore not a single trace of humanity nor any emotion that was discernibly human. This had to be Jaime Trenton, she thought.

Why am I here?? Kate wondered within.

The knifeman was closing in on her now only a few feet her junior in distance. He was slashing at her for all he was worth bringing the knife down with murderous rage each slash cutting the air more deeply than the last, closer, nearer still to her ear.

She wanted to deliver one of her signature spinning heel kicks and drop him, but no such luck, not in this place and not with these wounds, it wasn't possible.

"JESUS CHRIST"!!! She yelled palm on her knee as she found herself back at the hospital again. There was an elevator in the distance and he was still behind her, closing in.

"GO"!!! She urged herself verbally as the nightmare man dreamily stalked her.

Somewhere in Kates mind a pendulum swinging in darkness, Lillys face, voices and echoes from her own past meshing together, the chimes of night touching gingerly in the wind and a little river running downstream in the darkness.

Where were the doctors and nurses in this hospital?? Probably all dead. Kate surmised.

There was a matchbook on the floor. It said-The Bunny In Blue.

She looked over her right shoulder, his face was closer, stealing distance only four feet or so away. Who was Jaime Trenton and why did he want her dead?? Who had she been babysitting"?? Was any of this real or was this something that she saw only in her sleep??

The elevator doors opened and light poured out.

"Oh God"!!! She yelped, still not used to being a victim, for Kate Shamrock was accustomed to being the fearless heroine, not the person who was being victimized.

This has to be a figment of my imagination. She thought as she stole onto the elevator and watched the doors slam shut.

Five floors down the elevator came open again this time to silence and the softly falling rain outside of the emergency doors.

Where was he?? Had to be around here somewhere she registered making a mad dash toward the transparent glass for all she was worth, but when she got to the doors her feet inexplicably froze up on her and she couldn't move, as if suspended in time.

As if by invisible transport she suddenly found herself strolling the darkened streets of NIGHTS END again as strange men wearing sun glasses watched her from behind the windshields of passing cars, their gaze never off of her.

"What the fuck is going on"?? Shamrock asked, again met with silence and the whispering winds that were making laps around her.

"Don't fucking touch me". She hollered as a familiar looking Sheriff put his hand on her shoulder. "Everyone's entitled to one good scare". The Sheriff told her, but then, and without provocation he wrestled her to the ground and slapped a pair of bracelets on her. "You're under arrest for trespassing he said".

"Trespassing"?? Kate responded in a panic stricken, psychologically damaged voice. What exactly did he mean by trespassing?? She pondered again, another round of waking up, only this time in the presence of her sick and twisted Grandfather, Jonathan who was wearing a silk robe and matching hood. His flock stood around him, silent.

"Why am I here"?? Kate asked handcuffed to the back of a chair. There were hundreds of glowing television screens rooted in walls all around her, bleeding white light, no clear image discernible.

"You want me to answer that Kate?? Do you?? Why are you here?? You're here because I dreamt you here. I was cruel to your dead Uncle as a child, I even produced nightmares in his head that he never knew or could have known came from my unconscious mind.

When we lived at Bridge View Drive he told me about a nightmare that he had about there being two of me in a room, one who danced with

64

him and then traded places with the other who was sent to terrify him, the other wouldn't let him go even when he cried and begged to be freed, the other who dragged him into a darkened closet and held him there until he woke up screaming. I knew about the dream Kate, I knew about the dream even before he went to sleep the night before". Jonathan said motioning for someone to step out of a back room.

Soon they were joined by a man in a white mask, it was the same man who had been stalking her through NIGHTS END MEMORIAL HOSPITAL.

"This is Jaime Trenton". Jonathan boasted tying a gag around Kates mouth.

"NOOOO …… …… …… …… NOOOOO …… …… …… ……"
She screamed, but no one came to help her.

"When you're Uncle told me about the dream it was all I could do to keep the smirk off my face. How do you tell your three year old child that you implanted a nightmare in his head"??

The words "DREAMLESS SLEEP" flashed somewhere, pink neon against a black back drop in her head.

"You know what's on the monitors that you see all around this room"?? The Dreamless Sleep asked.

"Childrens nightmares, as well as other atrocities that my people and I are privy to, atrocities that we create, a bad dream for the children. We use dreams to kill Kate, but you don't have to worry, because you're going to become one of us". Jonathan said binding Shamrocks ankles to the chair.

"FUCK YOUUUUUU"!!!!!!!! She managed, struggling against her bindings. "NOOOOOOO"!!!!!!!!

On one of the monitors Kate saw Lilly Chicoines face, her lips producing a silent monologue as if she was blissfully unaware that she was being watched or recorded. The footage looked to be from somewhere in the night on Ontario Street.

Jonathan Dane was standing in the centre of the room with his arms outstretched mugging for the series of cameras that watched him.

"We're sick Kate, we're sick"!!! The Dreamless Sleep said before a wall of flames engulfed her vision. When her vision, sight inside returned, the man in the mask who had helped her was doing battle with Jaime Trenton as Jonathan Dane darted for cover in an alcove.

There were a series of kicks and punches between the masked man and Jaime Trenton before Jaime Trenton slashed at the man in the mask who disarmed the nightmare man and turned his own knife against him powering the blade toward his chest, pushing, forcing, willing it to succeed in its destination, but the struggle would not end there as Jonathans men rushed to help Jaime.

"Clear". A voice said outside of any of this.

"Arghh"!!! The masked man managed finally gaining enough momentum to force the blade through Trentons eye, killing him.

"We got it". The voice outside said.

"We're gonna lose her". A nurse said handing a suture to the doctor who was attempting to close Kate up.

"She's flat lining" ... ... "Hit her with the paddles".

"All clear".

Now, in NIGHTS END the masked man was driving Kate away from the city limits as she slept in the passenger seat, dreaming, her head swimming between here and there, wherever there was, and Jonathan Danes men were gaining on them, making headway.

"She's back". Dr. Kissinger said. "She's breathing on her own".

The nurse and the other attendants in the operating theatre were smiling, pleased that they had not lost their famous patient. "Okay, close her up". One of the assisting Surgeons ordered.

There was a metallic clink as someone dropped a hollow point bullet in a dish with a pair of tweezers.

"She's gonna make it". Dr. Tarrell assured.

Outside of the O.R., Andrew Dane, Ray, and a wheelchair bound Leilani sat in terrified silence as they waited for the results of Kates surgery. It had been all night plus a few hours, but no news was good news, it was better than hearing what they feared the most or Christ only knew what else. Kate had been very lucky, she had received a bullet in the head through the drivers side window of her car as she headed back home from the hospital after seeing Leilani, and then all holy hell had broken loose.

"Good news, she's gonna make it". Dr. Karen Tarrell said emerging from the O.R. with her surgeons mask dangling from around her neck. She was smiling. "There's even better news. No permanent damage".

"Nope, not to her". Ray said seriously with his chin and eyes facing the floor. He was going to murder these motherfuckers gangland style and then take off, whatever the set of circumstances.

Andrew Dane was sobbing now as he cradled his wifes head, his cheeks were puffy and red and his eyes blood shot. Ray was wondering where he was going to get a gun around here, bullets, and a vest.

"Oh my God". Andrew sobbed as he began to break down completely.

Then, someway, somehow she was back in that place. They had done it, they had managed to run Jonathan Danes men off the road into a shadowy ditch, two of them dead behind the wheel. Now the sun was coming up and she and the masked man were driving away, far away, from NIGHTS END.

CHAPTER III

A t this time I want to take a moment to address the people around the world with phobias who suffer in silence every day. As a person who shares your affliction I know what it is to wake throughout the night and in the morning with terrors and anxiety and to live in fear and ridicule every day from those who are wicked enough, and evil enough, to take advantage of us. I have been there since 2012 when my nightmare began. I also want you to know that it is important for you to talk to someone, a Family member, a friend, or a trusted confidant. It is important that you share your fears with someone so that your panic and anxiety doesn't eat you alive, and so that there are others who know and understand what you're going through.

What I have learned since 2012 is that PHOBIC PEOPLE are a special group who deserve special recognition from the public, and not the kind of recognition that includes mocking, ridicule, or being taken advantage of in such a way that those who are aware of our affliction are attempting to use it for personal gain or leverage. NO ONE HAS A RIGHT TO TREAT YOU OR YOUR ILLNESS WITH SUCH DISREGARD!!!!! ... ... NO ONE!!!!!!!!!

At the culmination of this manuscript I will be working with a group of individuals to ensure, or to at least attempt to assure that people such as us do not suffer in silence anymore. I am going to work toward having a special 24hr. HOTLINE set up so that those of us who live in fear and are afraid to open up, or have no one to open up to, will have a place where their voice can be heard.

We should not have to suffer in silence anymore.

Sincerest Regards,
David Dane Wallace/Von "The Icon"
Author

On the morning of her release Kate Shamrock was wheeled out of the hospital and into the side door of an armoured van by her Father who was flanked by two personal security guards that he himself had handpicked, only the best, highly trained and extremely dangerous.

They were in the underground parking lot now in a special section of the hospital waiting for clearance from the guard in the booth upstairs who would signal them when it was time to go. There was no air down here, shadows and the vapours left behind by the previous occupants gas tanks.

"Okay". Kevin radioed from the booth amidst drumbeats of static.

"Let's roll". Cole Gillespie responded through the mic that was clipped to his shirt. He wore a black suit, sun glasses, and an ear piece. Kate thought that he looked like he should be guarding the main man, and at a time, he had.

"I don't need all of this shit". Kate protested in the direction of her Father who was seated directly behind her beside the second of the two body guards whose name was Darrell Sea. He also wore a black suit and a pair of wrap around sun glasses. He looked more like a standard, you cross me and I'll snap your neck type of guy, no patience, fuck with me and you're dead. He was also Irish, which accounted for his hair trigger temper, just give me a reason.

"Nice to meet you". He said extending his hand to the legendary Shamrock. "I know who you are. It's an honor". He said moving his lower jaw around as if it was under pressure.

"Likewise". Kate said, not giving in. She was afraid of nothing and didn't need nor want to be protected. She WAS NOT A VICTIM!!!

As they reached the street, rain blew about in dancing gusts making visibility more difficult than normal. It had been eight weeks since she had been shot, and since Donovan and Jill had been lowered into the ground. She had attended neither funeral and would NEVER forgive herself for it, horrible circumstances or not, there was in her mind, no excuse. She loved them both and felt that it should have been her who had been killed as opposed to either one of them. Why should she have lived when she had been the target of the assassin or assassins??

"Someone tried to kill you". Andrew commented. "I'm not just gonna leave my own Daughter unprotected under circumstances like that".

"Turn here". Gillespie said pointing out the front window as his left foot rested on the edge of Kates wheel chair platform.

As the van rolled through a series of traffic lights Darrell pointed out a vehicle that he noticed in the rear view mirror. "I think we might've picked up a tail". He said in Cole Gillespies direction.

"You think it's fire fight time"?? Sea asked his partner and life long friend.

"I hope not".

"What, what's going on"?? Andrew Dane asked adjusting his blazer at the top.

"Maybe nothing. We'll have to wait and see". Gillespie replied.

As the van entered an alley way the would be tail disappeared down a side street and made a right.

"I guess it's not Happy Hour after all". Cole said.

"You know this guy"?? Cole asked showing Kate a photograph.

"Yeah, that's Dee Martine". She responded.

"He's a killer". Cole said. "He may be the man who killed your Uncle".

She was speechless now, as though someone had knocked the wind out of her. "Why would Dee kill Uncle Von"?? The gorgeous kick boxing titlist asked bewildered.

"There are a number of possibilities starting with the fact that Dee is known in the underworld as some who's involved in trafficking girls for the purpose of sex slavery. We have reason to believe that your Uncle may have known something that they wanted him to keep quiet about".

"Cole, why would Uncle Von have any information … … … … … … …

"No, no. We have reason to believe that some information was passed to him before he died and that he was killed for it". Sea explained. "Your Uncle was a hero, and now here's something that you don't know. We knew your Uncle".

Kate frowned quizzically. "How do you guys know Uncle Von"?? She asked.

"Cause we lived in the same block". Darrell answered doing the lower jaw thing again.

There was traffic now, heavy and steady, off rooting them by several blocks.

"Get someone to come in behind us". Cole ordered into the mouth piece of the two way radio he was holding. "Christ, you can't count on anyone for anything anymore". He said as a hail of bullets erupted from somewhere beside the van. "Get your head down". Gillespie ordered forcing Kates head low with his hand. "Shit"!!! He hollered.

"They're not piercing the vehicle so we're lucky that they didn't come well prepared". Sea commented.

"Who's doing this"?? Andrew asked.

"We think they're eastern quadrant, but that's all we know". Cole responded, un holstering his fire arm. "And Dee Martine is involved".

"I hear sirens". Shamrock remarked pissed as hell that someone was making her a victim.

"DOWN"!!! Cole hollered as a series of hollow point rounds pierced the side windows of the van.

"GO"!!! He yelled in the direction of the driver who was trying to maneuver himself out of their current position in the lane as the vans engine roared.

Outside The Police were involved in a heavy fire fight with a group of well dressed assassins who were on bent knee firing off rounds from behind the cover of their car doors as the van sped off into an alleyway, burning rubber.

"What the fuck was that all about"?? Shamrock asked rattled but not scared. "These people are very determined". The fighter commented in a winded voice leaning up against the vans interior wall close to the wheel hub. "What the fuck did Uncle Von know?? One of these days I'm gonna make sure that tomorrow never comes for these lowlifes". She guaranteed looking in the direction of the ex Pro Boxer who was from The Maritimes.

"I don't know". Sea said, he was at least as seasoned as Shamrock but had retired his gloves many years ago. He was again doing the lower jaw thing, dancing it around.

"I want her taken to the safe house and watched round the clock". Gillespie ordered chambering his firearm. "Whoever wants you dead wants you dead very badly. These people just opened fire on The Police on a busy street in broad daylight. I'd say they've made their point". He said truthfully.

"Where's the safe house"?? Andrew asked.

"Upper Westmount, we have guards posted there". Cole assured, closing his blazer as he up righted himself. "Take a right here". He ordered the driver as they turned North heading toward Sherbrooke West.

"Fuck, I wish we didn't have to keep going. I'd rather fight these people on the ground". Sea said honestly, he was through being the hunted, something that he didn't have the temperament for, to Irish, and to damn hot blooded.

"That's noble of you". Cole said with a trace of a grin on his face. "This is for you". He said passing a firearm to "The Immortal" Von "The Icons" kid Brother. "Von would've wanted you to have this". He said, grinning again.

"I fuckin hate these things, but if it means the difference between my Daughters life and death then I guess it's necessary". The straight laced never off the book Andrew Dane said examining the firearm on top of the rag that it had been presented to him on.

"You'll need this to". Cole Gillespie informed him passing along a sheet of paper with extensive writing on it.

"What's this"?? Andrew asked.

"Temporary permit, we acquired it for you yesterday".

Andrew was nodding now as the van sped into the driveway and drove around to the rear of the house toward a waiting Leilani Dane who had fully healed.

"I'll help you get down from there". Darrell offered reaching for Kate Shamrock who almost couldn't stand up as the van came to a complete halt.

"All clear". Cole mouthed into the walkie-talkie.

"I can't believe any of this". Andrew Dane commented barely half awake. The Police would likely be here soon rolling up the driveway and by God enough was enough, he wanted out of this mess so badly he could taste it.

"I'll go check the perimeter". Darell said, although he was more than reasonably certain that had already been done.

"I don't want the fuckin wheelchair". Kate "The Gate" said pushing past the two wheeled rolling monster that sat to her left. The fuckin thing wreaked of sweat and she wondered who had been renting it out before her.

"You need to conserve your strength". The high powered Andrew Dane warned her.

"Yeah, well I'll conserve it some other way. I don't want that miserable piece of rolling crap anywhere near me". She pledged, right as rain. She had inherited her stubborn disposition from her old man, no one was going to tell her what to do nor how to do it. It would take more than a little piece of lead to destroy Kate "The Gate" Shamrocks will or cerebral endurance. She hadn't become a champion by lying down, attitude and bad to the fucking bone, just like Lilly whose memory she cherished.

"All clear". Darrell said returning from his rounds.

"Roof"!!! WARRIOR barked sprinting around to the back of the house where Kate immediately bent down to greet him. "I was wondering where you had disappeared to". The seasoned titlist said showering the Adorable Dogo with a barrage of hugs and kisses.

"Roof". He intoned a second time as he basked in the glow of the attention that he was receiving. "Aww ... ... I love you sweetie". Kate said kissing WARRIOR fully on the snout.

He was jubilant, loving every moment that he was shown love.

Just then there was the sound of sirens somewhere in the distance moving closer like rolling thunder.

"Fuck, here come the cowboys". Kate said turning slightly away from WARRIOR as she continued to stroke his thick cranium with one hand.

He was moaning pleasurably now, as if proud that he was so well loved.

That was the nature of The Dogo, they had terrific pride.

As the Police filtered in droves up the driveway Andrew Dane came around to greet them wishing to holy hell that he was anywhere other than here.

"Everything alright"?? One of Montreals finest asked sticking his head out the window of the car.

"Everything's more than fine". Darrell Sea said paralleling the cruiser with his legs. "We have everything in hand here". He said tapping two fingers on the hood of the black and white.

MONICA-

You and you alone gave birth to this nightscape, to this experience, and to this one of a kind story. I may have written it, but always with you as inspiration in mind and in heart. Aside from my two year old precious niece Kate, you are the most special person who has ever come into my life, bar none. I loved and love you as I have no other on this planet, nor anywhere else in this solar system. MY NUMBER ONE BUNNY, FOREVER AND ALWAYS.

Von

WARRIOR-Daddy wants to take this time out to thank you for all of your contributions to this book, because without your sacrifices, without all of the mornings and afternoons that you gave up, no part of this manuscript would have been possible.

You sat in patiently on many a muggy afternoon with your legs dangling over the edge of our couch and your tongue hanging out cheerfully as you kept vigilant of the moment when we'd be going out for one of our WARRIOR WALKS. You are the most loving animal I have ever known, along with the late, legendary, HUNTER WOOF. Daddy loves you buddy. Thank you for always being by my side. I vow to always be by yours.

Daddy

MUM-I want to thank you for all of your recent contributions to WARRIORS life and happiness. We both appreciate it.

MY DOGO WARRIOR ON THE GRASS

MY DOGO WARRIOR

MY DOGO WARRIOR LOUNGING ON THE COUCH!!!

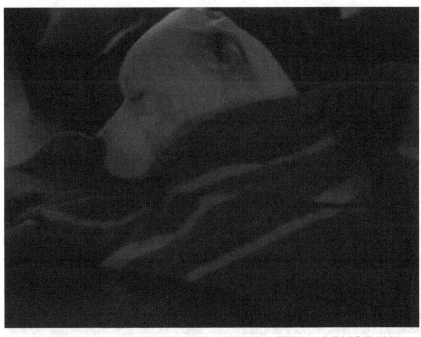

MY DOGO WARRIOR SOUND ASLEEP AFTER A LONG DAY!!!

MY DOGO WARRIOR CURLED UP ON THE COUCH-
THE MOST ADORABLE K-9 IN THE WORLD

MY NEIGHBOURHOOD, JUST OFF FULLUM

My constant companion WARRIOR

Ontario Streets Original Gangster

Ontario Streets Last Outlaw

The Knife of Thug Life

THE ONTARIO STREET ORIGINAL

A MORE DANGEROUS PART OF FRONTENAC

Ontario Streets Rocky Balboa

THE BACK ALLEYS OF ONTARIO STREET

NEARBY PARK BY NIGHT

PART II

AND THE DEAD SHALL RISE

"It's him, Daddy, it's him"!!! Kate hollered waking from fitful sleep in tears with dappled imprints from the leaves outside dancing in synchronization on her pillow.

"It's who baby. What are you talking about"?? Andrew asked embracing his Daughter as he would've when she was still a child. He had heard her scream from all the way down the hallway. He had nearly broken his neck climbing out of bed to run to her rescue.

"It's Uncle Von, he's still alive. I saw him in my dream". She cried feverishly. "It was him, in the mask downstairs that night. He saved us from those men. He's been watching over us".

"Oh my God". Andrew said raising his eyebrows slightly. "Your Uncle, my Brother, is dead". He said emotionally.

Kate was shaking her head argumentatively now, some of her medication still taking hold. She had a battery of prescriptions in her system.

"He was still alive in my dream. I know it was him downstairs, and in Nights End". She said her face flushed and tears, hot to the touch. "I know it in my heart Daddy. He's still alive". She said of her Immortal Hero.

"Aw God, Kate, your Uncle is dead, you know that".

She was shaking her head rebelliously again, and for a moment Andrew thought that she resembled Lilly via expression, her way or the highway. There was only one of both.

"What's wrong sweetheart"?? Leilani said standing in the light of the doorway.

"Kate thinks that my Brother's still alive".

"Uncle Von's alive Daddy, you'll see". Kate insisted.

Shadows.

The next night under the cover of darkness Kate Shamrock stole into the grave yard where they had buried her Uncle with a satchel of tools over her shoulder and a will of iron in her gut. There were no trespassers other than her, she owned the night. She hadn't brought any I.D. for fear she got arrested and disgraced herself as well as her Family. This would be an unspeakable headline-Bereaved Niece Digs Up Uncles Tomb-News At Eleven!!!

"Let's give it a shot". Kate said lifting a shovel by its handle and beginning to dig a giant hole scooping dirt to her left with both hands as a flashlight sat adjacent her Uncles grave illuminating every stroke of her excavation.

Somewhere the wind howled beyond a hill and then sighed in a downward spiral as it leveled off like a smothered fire burning down to even settled ash.

It had to have been him because it couldn't have been anyone else, that or she was just plain fuckin nuts, one or the other. Either way, she would know soon enough. Half an hour and she'd be done, coming closer to the inside of darkness.

Where would I be if I wasn't here?? Kate wondered in order to pass the time.

As she got closer to the box she noticed a monochrome blue mist blowing in gusts across the length of the Cemetery in shallow streams of vapour.

"You have to be down here Uncle Von. I don't work for free". She gasped driving the metal end of the shovel right through the roof of the coffin.

"YES!!! YES"!!! She celebrated emotionally". "Empty". She said as a tall hulking shadow appeared at the side of the hole.

"Looking for me"?? Dee asked whacking her in the cranium with one of her own digging instruments before her vision turned to blackness.

Before Kate had awoken from the blow to the head, a man sat in a darkened room before a bank on monitors, each demonstrating a different profile of Dee Martine standing in the night. The hour, and the moment was almost upon them, the moment when the truth would finally be told, and the world would finally know what had really happened.

"It's time to go". An official looking gentlemen said from two feet behind him. "He has Kate you know".

The man in the mask was clenching his fists as he stared in the direction of the glowing monitors. His breathing was laboured, as if radiating its own form or palpable anger, it was almost tangible.

"The leer jet will be ready in thirty minutes. We fly to Montreal in an hour. It's time to give the world back their hero". The Official said before stepping back out of the room.

"Because your Uncle was, and is nothing to me. You know that I knew his wife, and I knew Jenny to, until she saw something that she wasn't supposed to see and I had to give her some chloroform and dump her in the harbour". The seven foot tall Dee said shooting footage of Kate as her head lolled to one side as she sat bound to a chair.

"Do you even know where the fuck you are you stupid bitch"?? Dee asked as the glare bled from the spotlight above them. "This is streaming all over the world right now, and when you wake up completely I'm going to make you feel so much pain that you'll beg me to kill you".

"Mggrhh" ... ... Kate cried, already in agony.

"There are thousands on Ontario Street tonight only seconds from here because you know what day today is?? It's November 7th, the anniversary of Lilly Chicoines death. They don't have their heroes anymore, no more Von "The Icon" and no more Lilly "Bad To The Bone" Chicoine, and if by chance your Uncle did make it out of that cross bow situation alive, I'm going to kill him this time". Martine assured spewing venom in the small room that seemed deprived of oxygen.

As he said this a black Dodge Viper purred into the centre of the gathered crowd on Ontario Street stopping directly in front of the sleepy community centre windows and killed its lights.

Somewhere in the dark, LULLABY, BY LEGENDARY ROCK GROUP NICKELBACK BLASTED HYPNOTICALLY THROUGH THE NIGHT AS THE PASSENGER DOOR OF THE VIPER CAME OPEN ... ...

"OH MY GOD"!!! Tiffany said as an all too familiar figure stepped into the night dressed in a black T-Shirt, blue jeans, and cut gloves.

"IT'S VON "THE ICON"!!! Someone hollered as the frenzied crowd burst into a mixture of sobs, cheers and tears. It was like watching Jesus Christ return to Jerusalem.

In an underground room, held captive, Kate "The Gate" Shamrock was watching all of this on a monitor as tears rolled down her beautiful cheeks. "I love you"!!! She sobbed, deeply emotional.

"WHAAAT"!!!! DEE fumed. "I'll kill you you fucker"!!! He shouted almost knocking himself off balance as he kicked over an empty paint can and bolted down the hallway of the shady apartment complex where he had rented a single room.

Outside in the darkness "The Immortal" VON "THE ICON" barrelled through the adoring crowd to a series of loud cheers and a chant of WE LOVE YOU!!! WE LOVE YOU!!! WE LOVE YOU!!! As the glare from the haunting overhead vapour lamps bounced off of his sun glasses. Canadian flags sailed patriotically in the wind, rippling, flapping, and dancing as if in sync as if part of the show. ONTARIO STREETS HERO had come home and was now here to fight for them once more.

Shimmers filled the twilight as DEE collided with VON "THE ICON" who immediately met his onslaught with a series of violent blows to the chest as VONS sun glasses bounced against the ground.

"CAN-A-DA"!!! "CAN-A-DA"!!! The crowd chanted roaring approval as VON hit DEE in the kidneys with a series of body blows causing the big Romanian to buckle and fold slightly as he petered backward, petered backward, back peddling!!!

"WE LOVE YOU!!! WE LOVE YOU"!!! The chant rang out.

"MR. MAGNUM, MR. MAGNUM"!!! Rey shouted from the edge of Vons vision as Dee floored Ontario Streets Hero with a violent fist to the face. "Hit him Mr. Magnum"!!! Rey cheered. "Fuck him up"!!! Rey hollered bringing the night in around them with bursts of emotion.

It was all coming back in a whirl wind now. He could feel the night again, time and again, walking into The Domino and seeing Lilly sitting there, giving her a quiet kiss on the lips in the middle of the night, his Uncle standing proudly and patriotically wearing the Canadian flag over his uniformed shoulders at the head of a twenty one gun salute. Tom Wallace had once trained commandos.

"Love yah son". He heard Thomas say before his favourite Uncle saluted him underneath the threshold of a doorway, medals and Canadian National Pride glinting hypnotically. Tom Wallace had been a Canadian Treasure and Hero to his nation, a true representative of the flag.

The Canadians were on their feet now, waving flags.

"I love you forever Lilly". Von said answering Dees punches with a barrage of punches to the face, and indeed he did. Lilly would forever and always be the love of his life, with no equal and no competitor. One and only.

"He's gonna fall". Someone shouted from the sidelines.

"MR. MAGNUM, FINISH HIM"!!! Rey hollered as he shadow boxed against the air.

Dee was staggering now, wiping the cob webs off of his face with one hand.

"GO TO SLEEP"!!! THE IMMORTAL VON "THE ICON" shouted as he hit DEE below the chin with a violent upper cut sending him crashing back first into the grill of a dairy truck, bloodied, concussed, bent, and unable to continue.

"Uncle Von"!!! Kate yelled power walking toward her favourite Uncle with tears in her eyes, she had escaped her captors bindings and was now hobbling toward her Fathers older sibling covered in a heavy sheen.

"I love you, I love you Uncle Von". She sobbed melting into the arms of her hero who was bleeding from the nose, forehead and lip.

"David and Goliath". Someone shouted as helicopter propellers whirred amidst swooning spotlights over the darkened neighbourhood as Ontario Streets conquering hero and his niece embraced as legendary photographer Luigi snapped a photo of them together. "That's gonna turn out well". The high class French Italian gentlemen said.

"Thanks Luigi". Von said as Ray smiled proudly in the direction of his former flat mate.

"Why did you let us think you were dead"?? Kate asked breaking down again, overwhelmed with emotion.

"Your safety. We thought we could protect you that way. A friend of mine saw something that she wasn't supposed to see. They killed her for it". Von said as two of Montreals finest, station 22, hooked Dee up and loaded him into the back of a Police van.

"Mr. Magnum". Ray exclaimed as his old friend stepped away from his nieces embrace.

"Mr. Dee is an asshole".

"Sanctuary, his name is Sanctuary". Von explained. "He's an assassin, he also runs human trafficking operations. CSIS has a jacket on him a mile long".

"It's so good to have you back Brother". Ray said.

"Thanks Ray. It's good to see you man". Von said moving over to his Brother who had just shown up on the scene, his face was wet with tears.

"We thought you were gone forever". Andrew said breaking down.

"It's like they say, bad pennies have a way of turning up". Von exclaimed as Andrew embraced his older brother who was receiving pure adoration from The Ontario Street crowd.

"They love you here". Andrew observed with a light smile.

"Yeah, well, I love them to". Von said waving to the crowd as he nodded THANKS.

LULLABY BY NICKELBACK PLAYED ON.

"Jenny sent me a flash drive. This is what they wanted to kill you for".

"What's on the flash drive"?? Kate asked.

"Names, even footage of some girls being beaten and tortured by their captors. Faces, Jenny was one of them". Von went on. "She was helping them run one of their operations down to the last detail until she couldn't handle it anymore".

"So why didn't she just leave"?? Kate asked, half expecting the answer that was forthcoming.

"This isn't a burger joint, you don't just get up and walk out. Jenny tried to black mail her way out. They probably tortured her to get what you're holding in your hand". Von said as Kate unconsciously examined the device that had been placed in the center of her palm.

"So you faked your own death"??

"No, not exactly". Von continued as Ray remained silent, listening. "The sonovabitch actually hit me with an arrow. I was in a hospital for a while, that's when I realized the depth of the situation".

"So what happened"?? Ray asked, finally speaking up.

"I called an old friend of Thomas's but I didn't give him the device. I kept it as an insurance measure".

"So then why didn't you then"?? She asked bewilderment masking her features in this room full of night.

"Because what you're holding between your thumb and forefinger is going to keep them from killing us". Von said handing Ray a name and a number.

"Mr. Magnum, it's good to have you back". Ray said reaching out to embrace his old friend who reciprocated the hug. "It's good to have you back. I missed you". Von said sincerely.

"Where were you all this time"?? Shamrock asked.

"I was in Ottawa staying in a converted warehouse slash auto parts garage on Gladstone. I kept having these strange dreams about Rottweilers. The place was eerie enough by itself. I used to live in the area so out of a selection, I chose that location".

"WARRIOR will protect you from the Rottweilers". Kate said.

There were tears in Von "The Icons" eyes now. He had missed the adorable Dogo who had once filled his days and his heart with love. "Where is my Dog"?? He asked.

"He's at the safe house with Mom and Dad. He'll go crazy when he sees you". Kate remarked beaming from ear to ear.

"Call your Father and tell him to chauffeur him over here".

Just then Ramonds phone lit up. "Just wait a second. I have to take this". He said stepping out of the room momentarily. "Yeah, yeah". He said to whomever was on the other end of the call.

"I have to go". He said when he stepped back into the room. "I'll be back in a few days".

"Alright. Thanks for everything Rey". The Ontario Street Original said once again embracing his old friend and roommate.

"I have to go". Ray said.

"I'll see you on the other side of the moon". Von said smoothly as Ray stepped away from their embrace and vanished out the door ... ...

The next morning when Von "The Icon" awoke from his deep sleep he noticed a large white Dog wrapped in a bow seated at the foot of his bed.

"Hey, how you doin"?? Ontario Streets Last Outlaw asked with a wide grin on his face.

WARRIOR groaned as if to say "Hello" in dog language as Von grabbed him and wrestle hugged him to the mattress as he showered The Adorable Dogo with kisses.

"MMrds" ... ... WARRIOR managed which was DOGO for I missed you, I love you.

"I love you to buddy". Von said planting a series of kisses on WARRIORS snout.

"Do you want some breakfast"?? Von asked standing up and stretching as his muscular frame rippled beneath the shirt that he had worn to bed.

"Where do they keep the food around here anyway"?? He asked, still trying to clear the cob webs away.

It was temperately cool outside, and The Ontario Street Original could feel the draft seeping in through the crack in the window.

"That my phone"?? He asked aloud remembering that he had forgotten to charge it last night.

"Hello". He answered into the mouth piece. "Hey Damian, how you doin"?? And then there was a response on the other end. "Yeah, I'm a bit dizzy. Give me half an hour, I need to feed WARRIOR and grab a quick shower". He said. "Yeah, where at?? Alright, alright. I'll meet you at the spot".

"I heard about last night. So you managed". Damian said. He was standing at a pay-phone outside of a seedy tavern with a broken window in the front.

"I don't know how many more times they're gonna let me do this".

"How many more times who's gonna let you do this"??

"Whoever owns the eternal clock. Something tells me that I've used up a lot of favors".

"They keep coming as long as you know how to play the game right. I should know. I over dosed six times".

"They have to like you to let you walk away that many times".

"You think so"??

"That's what I hear".

"Okay listen, do what you have to do and then come and say hi. I'll see you soon".

"Ciao". Von. said flipping his phone shut.

When Von got there he found Damian in a state of disrepair, high, slightly drunk and in need of stitches in his forehead. "Hey, what the hell happened to your face"?? He asked.

"Loan sharks, I owe them a lot of money and they're tired of me not paying them back".

"You're lucky you didn't ask for a raise". The Knife Of Thug Life said not meaning to make light of the situation.

"Yeah, no kidding, I believe it".

"That needs attention". Von said of the gash on his friends forehead.

"I wish, I can't go to a hospital right now, i'm fuckin sick. I haven't done a hit since last night".

Von was well aware that no medical facility would offer any assistance to Damians current predicament laced with the fact that he'd be pushed back to last priority.

"What are the two of you doing around here"?? A Police Officer asked from the window of the cruiser that had just rolled up on them. "You're the guy who writes the books". The Badge commented growing noticeably affable at the realization of who his audience was, at least half of it. "What happened to his forehead"?? The French Beat Cop asked.

Dane, who had been hassled before, was also French. His late Grand Mother had been Doris Marie Le Blanc from Annapolis Royal, Nova Scotia. Her Mother, Marie, was as French as it got, and French had been Doris's first language. Doris had lived with Dane for most of his life off and on until the day they buried her. Her Husband, Tom, Danes Grand Father, had been a rugged old Scotsman.

"That needs attention". The Cop said of the wound on Damians forehead.

"Yeah, I told him that". Ontario Streets Last Outlaw said.

"Fuckin Drug Dealer this guy". The Badge hammered.

"Hey, don't you have a bunch of speeding tickets to hand out"?? The fighter asked as the cops expression began to sour. He was pissed that this guy was hanging out with a known dealer at all, he felt like running both of them in just to make a point, but then there might be a public outcry.

"Alright, get him out of the area, we don't wanna see him around for a while.

Déjà vu, Von thought.

"C'mon let's go". Von urged his friend who was staring at the cop unconsciously.

As the cruiser began to pull away the two of them continued down the street in this seedy area that was not Ontario Street, but that was beginning to sharply resemble it.

"It was nice of them to stop and say high, I think". Damian said.

"That's what they get paid for. Where would we be without six nine to five"?? Von said stepping on the cigarette that Damian had dropped. "You need to have that looked at".

"I don't have time, seriously".

"If that's a concuss … … … … … …

"Hey, that's one of the guys that I owe money to". Damian said scanning the other side of the street. He had noticed one of Maxes employees over by the park with the stage in it. Max was the loan shark.

"Yeah, maybe you should get lost for a while". Von warned, thinking of his very first impression of the guy who stood next to him. Damian was the bad influence standing in the shadows of the arcade waiting for all the naïve young girls to show up and buy drugs from him, the ones who had run away from home or been warned by their mothers to stay away from guys like him. He was without a doubt every mothers worst nightmare come to life.

"HEY"!!! The muscular collector shouted from the foot of a wrought iron fence that encircled the perimeter of the huge park. "You're gonna get your neck broken".

"Hey, maybe you should learn to be a nicer person ye know". Von "The Icon" shouted back as Damian kept his back to what was going on not wanting to feel the effects of a beating for the second time in one morning.

"I don't think this end of town likes you very much". The Icon remarked glancing at a dimly lit restaurant menu that sat on the other side of a pizza joint window. There was a sign above it that read-All Slices $2.99.

This had become the new red zone or halt light district. There were working girls on every corner or seated behind every open window. Aids had likely found a new home here. Von registered. There were syringes and condoms strewn along every gutter and thrown haphazardly on the ground of every alley way that wreaked of whatever foul odour. This place was becoming Ontario Street 2000 all over again. Had it not been for the frequent patrols, the neighbourhood would would have likely become a rival to Vancouvers down town east side, or D.T.S. as it was widely known, populated by transients looking for a place to stop over, do Heroin, pick up a girl, or even die.

The neighbourhoods other moniker was "Pain And Wastings" after its worst corner, Main and Hastings. Dane himself had worked The Black Hills in 1994 for a local Security firm, the place had been BAD, BAD back then, an evil half lit fucking nightmare full of societies worst drug addicts, but there was also something alluring about such venues, they had a way of capturing ones imagination and created great inspiration for books or film.

"You need to find a hobby, other than Heroin". Ontario Streets Immortal Hero said glancing in the direction of his rival turned friend.

"Yeah, I know, it's not so easy when you've been doing this for so long".

"Has anyone ever told you that you look like a Porcupine"?? Von asked taking stock of Damians naturally Spikey hair, his back ground was a mixture of French, Italian, Indian, French Quebecer, and Dane did not know what else.

"No, but I've been called a prick".

"Yeah, I think I remember calling you that once".

"Hey, you got a cigarette"?? A local street girl asked as she approached them with her hand outstretched.

"I had a pack, but I lost them when I was getting beat up". Damian responded.

Von said nothing, to busy keeping vigilant of the collector who had just hung up his cell phone. "We gonna do this right now"?? He asked with a weary expression on his face. They were being approached by two thugs who looked like they'd spent the better part of their thirty something years in a tattoo parlour.

"Do what"?? Damian asked, waking up.

"Whoa, whoa, whoa". Von said raising his palm in a halting gesture. Neither one of these guys looked like they'd been blessed with the virtue of patience.

The first of the two thugs said something to Damian in French before turning his attention to Von whose mood was darkening like a cinema before the start of a movie.

"You guys need to work out a payment plan". Von said half joking.

"This isn't Walmart". The second of the two thugs remarked, spewing a litany of French profanities in Damians direction. They were on their way to hitting him, again.

"Yeah, you start throwin punches and I'm gonna give you both some bruises of your own". The Ontario Street Original warned.

"One of them has a crow bar". Damians said in a low voice that was fueled with a palpable anxiety.

"If you hit em another time it's you that's gonna owe money". Von promised shaking out his left arm in one quick motion as the first of Maxes boys swung in his general direction. He didn't connect.

Just then The Police Cruiser reappeared and the two henchmen who worked for Max Caberera made themselves scarce quickly darting back across the street and down an alleyway.

"I thought I told you to get him outta here". The badge said.

"Did you say that"?? Von retorted.

"You see that. This is my life". Damian remarked". As the cop shook his head. He hadn't heard any of what Damian had to say, to busy fussing on his computer.

"Go home". He finally offered up, half paying attention.

Von nodded now lightly tapping Damian on the back of the shoulder.

"Let's go". He said.

"Jenny, was a street hooker that my Uncle Von knew. He thought initially that she had died of AIDS or a Drug overdose, but that turned out, not to be the case. She was in his first book, Urban Rain, and she was inducted into The Ontario Street Hall Of Fame in Neighbourhood Of Night. She looked like a young Michelle Pfeifer. She and my Uncle Von were very close. The last thing that Jenny ever said to my Uncle before she vanished was-I love you. She was standing in the sunset between two buildings. Then, one night, in the middle of the night while he was sleeping Uncle Von got a call from an Unknown number. It was Jenny. She was crying. She said that she was being forced to work for a bunch of people who Traffic Girls and that she couldn't take it anymore. I don't know what Uncle Von said to her.

Then, two days later Uncle Von got a delivery in the mail by special courier, it was the flash drive that he mentioned to you". Kate confided to Luigi who was a high class Italian Photographer who had become a friend of her Uncles. He was also extremely good looking for his age.

"Your Uncle, I can't believe he's alive". Luigi said brushing a speck of dust off of his jeans. "I mean, I'm grateful, I'm beyond grateful. I've enjoyed getting to know Von".

"My Uncle likes you to. Says you're 100% class".

"Well, I like your Uncle to". Luigi admitted. "I should be going. I have to go pick up a friend at the airport, he's flying in from Perugia tonight on The Red Eye". The World Class and highly sought after lens man said.

"Thanks very much for the meal and the conversation". Shamrock said as she collected a Champagne glass from the table top. They were in her Parents house.

"No, I'm the one who should be thanking you". Luigi Di Genova said. "It's an honor to have dinner with such an accomplished young woman. I've had a terrific evening. Thankyou". The kind and honorable Luigi said.

"Goodnight".

Sexxy Eddy gazed above him to see the heavy spotlights burning in a vapour over the sold out arena. Tonight, he would make his peace with the wrestling world, and with himself.

He would never be able to let go of what happened to Gabriel Sykes, never be able to forgive himself, but he also owed something to the thousands of adoring fans that he loved who had paid to come out and see him, and back stage, behind the black curtain that the wrestlers came through was a dear friend who had in his own right risen from the grave. "The Immortal" Von "The Icon", the leader and Father of The Ontario Street Originals, was in attendance.

It would take all of the courage that he ever thought he had to say the things that he needed to say. These people, the fans of this company had stood behind him and supported him in his time of need, and to Eddy Dorozowsky, the man, that had meant the entire world.

"Oh, God". Eddy began about to do the shoot (Unscripted interview), of his life. "First of all I'd give my life for this business". He said rubbing his hand over his face. "I truly love what I do.

I became a Professional Wrestler because I wanted to entertain people, I wanted to make people happy. This gig for me has always been about making other people feel good, about making all of you feel good." Eddy said making a line in the air with his finger in the direction of the hushed crowd. "But I failed each and every one of you, and what's worse, and I have remorse … … … … … … … … Eddy said doing his best to fight back tears as he again raised a hand to his face. "What's worse is that I failed Gabriel, who was a friend of mine, and I failed all of you. I don't deserve your love or respect, but you still give it to me anyway". He said, as the formerly hushed crowd broke into a chant of-EDDY!!! EDDY!!! EDDY!!!

"I don't deserve that". Eddy said again choking on his own tears as Ontario Streets Immortal Legend watched on from a backstage monitor.

"I took away Tamantha Sykes husband, Eddy said of the valet who was known in the business as Tamantha Evans.

"You gave me everything that I have". Eddy said looking over the crowd as he held the stick (Microphone) in his grip. "I owe my success in this business not to myself, not to any promotor, but to each and every one of you". Eddy said again panning across the crowd with his finger as the heat from the overhead vapour lamps beckoned like a Heaven from above. "I've never made this public until now. Right after Gabriels passing, I spent a few days alone on a desolate beach in Maui". The Pro Wrestling Icon said moving a short distance around the ring, his red parka and black leather pants ashine in the glow of the spot lamps.

"There was a moment where I thought that my life couldn't go on and I came very close to putting a pistol to my head and ending it. It was only because of this business, and because of all of you that I decided not to go through with what I was about to do, and this is not a part of the entertainment, this is completely off the work. It's not because I'm special, because there's nothing special about me, it's because you're special. Instead of you cheering for me, I should be cheering for you.

Thank you for making my life special". Eddy said laying the mic flat on the mat and exiting the ring below the golden vapour lamps that seemed to shine upon him from Heaven.

A hushed silence had again fallen over the crowd.

"I love you". Eddy mouthed walking one foot at a time down the steps and away from the ring.

As soon as Eddy reached the Gorilla Position he was greeted by "The Immortal" Von "The Icon" whose eyes were hidden behind a pair of black sun glasses that gave him a shady if not slightly sinister appearance. He immediately embraced his friend whispering something into his ear to which Eddy briefly nodded.

"Most incredible speech I've ever heard". Someone else commented.

Von thought that Eddy's mood seemed somehow off, tuned out, something not quite resonating properly. No more tears, too fast.

"Kate's here, she wants to see you". Von said smiling genuinely, decked out in a black T-Shirt, cut gloves and jeans with a black leather jacket. He looked lethal, Kate had commented on their way to the arena earlier. She had driven. The Immortal one did not drive, never had.

"Okay". Eddy said wiping whatever off of his lips. "I want a beer". Dorozowsky remarked at the same time that Von shot a glance in his pals direction. "No more beerless nights for me, and I want pussy".

The last comment was vintage him.

"I brought a couple of friends with me". Kate said appearing from the lobby of the back entrance.

"I'll bet they want autographs". Eddy commented flagging down a blond who was five to six feet from his reach. She was less than a ten but more than a nine.

Just then Scott Paris and Troy Barclay sauntered through a black curtain that hung from an overhang a few feet away, badass as ever, black jeans over skimpy leather vests, chiseled from stone. Not many could have gotten away with it.

Eddy was whistling his theme music now as the blond wrapped her stems around him. She recognized Von "The Icon" as the "HERO WHO HAD RISEN FROM THE DEAD"!!! That's what all of the new papers were printing.

"Hey Eddy". Kate said leaning in and pecking her Uncles friend on the cheek.

"Good to see you Kate". Eddy said at the same time, cradling the blonds ass cheeks in his sun tanned hands. "Sorry, I have my hands full right now". The Wrestling Superstar said bouncing Francines butt up and down in his hands.

"Long time". Von said cupping another wrestlers hand as he shook it.

"Someone needs to make a beer run". Scott Paris commented shadowing Vons position in the room.

Eddy turned his attention from the blond for a second to make eye to lens contact with Von. "How does it fuckin feel to come back from the grave"??

"Hey, isn't that Luigi over there"?? Kate asked accidently vetoing her Uncles response.

"Yeah, I think so". The Immortal one answered glancing across the room in the direction of catering.

Luigi Di Genova had done the ringside shoot for the entire show, now more than ever happy that he'd chosen the gigs that he had. He had gotten to meet so many interesting personalities, and tonights venue had been no exception. He was being showered with compliments on his work not to mention meeting some of the most unique characters that he had ever encountered.

"Von". He said approaching The Immortal one, and embracing him in the way that old friends embrace each other. "I can't tell you how happy I am that you're still alive". He said pulling Kate forward into the embrace.

"Yeah, well I'm not". A flashy blond body builder with curly hair said as he interrupted their reunion.

"Who the hell are you"?? Luigi asked, perplexed as the three way embrace broke off.

"I'm an old friend". The scumbag said lifting his shirt to expose a six pack and a chest full of black tattoos.

"That's not true". Von encouraged the interloper who was also a former training partner of his. "I never really liked you that much".

The guy in front of him had gotten heavily into Coke and messed his life up years ago, gone to prison, and stabbed a man to death in front of a parked car although it wasn't provable in court, although everyone knew that he had done it. It had taken a lot, and more than this piece of shit had in him, to stay clean.

"There are no drug dealers in this building. You might wanna try someplace else". Von elaborated.

"I'll stab you in the fuckin mouth". Brian threatened exposing the handle of a switch blade that rested neatly below his shirt.

"That's no way to greet someone who might kill you for less than you've already said". Von remarked, cool as ice.

Fuck's his problem?? Di Genova wondered staring at Brian as one would a vile piece of garbage. "He has no class". DiGenova remarked waving Brian off with his right hand.

Eddy was watching on now, wearing the faintest hint of a smirk.

"Alright Brian". Von said as if encouraging the games to commence as he held one hand slightly above the other as Brian Richie took a stab at his target.

"Fuck you, you … … … … … … … Kate said doing her Uncle a favor and clearing away the knife with a stealth, picture perfect spinning back kick.

"BITCH"!!! Brian hollered, as Von turned him backward by the neck and dropping both himself and Brian to the concrete at the same time with a thud. "I'll bet that stung". He said as he saw blood seep from a gash at the back of Brians head. He then stood up.

"You mother … … … … … … Brian said as he rose to his feet in an attempt to finish the fight, but it was too late, security had made their way to the back of the building and were now apprehending the fool who had caused the problem.

Eddys smirk had vanished like smoke into darkness.

"That was nice". One of the other wrestlers spoke up. "Where'd you learn that"?? He asked.

"I've been a Pro Wrestling Fan for thirty five years and you guys think I've never learned any of the tricks that you guys know"?? The Knife Of Thug Life asked.

"Happy for you, Mr. Magnum". Ray said showing up very un-expectedly.

"How'd you get in here"?? Von asked, smiling.

"I killed a sec-ur-ity guard". Ray said in his thick African accent that was one of his trademarks as well as part of his charm.

"Are you sure he's dead"?? Von asked. "Because we don't want any of his friends coming after you". He said within clear shot of two of the back up Security Guards who were still on the floor. They were laughing now to.

"The guy's O.D.ing". A woman with a backstage pass around her neck yelled as she came into the room.

"What"?? Von yelled, his smile now dead.

There were a flurry of whispers now circling the room.

"Where is he"?? Von asked eyes darting back and forth.

"Back door". Someone else answered.

"Someone call a doctor". Von shouted.

"He's gone". One of the Senior Security Officers said releasing the button on the side of his radio.

CHAPTER IV

Monica- You'll never know how hard it's been living each day without you. You meant everything to me, and without you it's like there's a piece of my life that I can't put back together. Each and every woman that I meet is simply nothing next to the real life Bad Ass that you always were. We were meant to know one another, and meant to be together. You breathed life into this genre for a nation, and a world of readers.

I still remember the energy that you brought to these streets. You were an original, and an Ontario Street Original. One of my motivations for exposing your real name to my readers is so that at the end of this book, you can finally be properly inducted into THE ONTARIO STREET HALL OF FAME by your real name. Monica Medeiros Abbona-Street Angel, and Hard Core Icon.

I love you always Baby Bunny … … … … … … … Von!!!

I want my life back, and I'm speaking here outside of this book. My life has been taken away from me by a flock of scavengers who want nothing more than to use every fear and phobia that's been instilled in me for their personal gain. Lowlife jack offs, pathetic pieces of shit.

Ever since 2012, it's been, what can I get by abusing or instilling phobias … … … … … … …

This vindicator in the night will one day swallow you WHOLE!!!

I have suffered and sacrificed immeasurably for the sake of a bunch of putrid filth who should by all rights be put out of their misery.

It is only the lowest of the low, as one who would steal a blind mans cane or a deaf mans hearing aid who would abuse someone who is a known phobic. Have you no remorse, no fear of reprisal??

What loathsome bitch gave birth to such future bastards??

Then you mock me by trying to group me as a crazy, that which this Legendary Hero is anything but, only for the sake of watching writhing, pitiless, snakes salivate as they hiss and pant dreaming of my demise. How far this country has fallen from grace, and tumbled to rubble.

You have taken me far down a dark and seemingly endless road, but I will return, I will come back from your black hearted, injurious methods of treachery and treason.

I remember being a human being who once had peace of mind and understood the comforts of happiness, but that moment has passed and I now must deal with all of you who have passed my phobias from one to another like a Family heir loom.

I will return, and much like my character, I will be The Conquering Hero!!!

Regards,
"The Immortal" Von "The Icon"

As Dane entered his dream he was walking over a footbridge in Ottawa with lights to either side of it. As he came to the side that bordered Somerset and Wellington he encountered a punkish girl, rail thin, wearing a musicians hat on her head and bruises over her eyes and face. Her name, her name something or other that began with an "N".

She was crying. Upon greeting her she explained that her 6'3 boyfriend who owned a gun had beaten her black and blue causing her to end up in the hospital for four days. "N" also explained that her dog was going to be euthanized by The S.P.C.A. if she did not go and claim him.

"My girlfriend did what you do". Dane told her, proudly displaying the image of URBAN RAINS stylish jacket that was on his screen saver.

"You must have money". The girl responded.

"Nope, I just get by". Dane had responded, at the time hardly feeling like he had ever been Von "The Icon" at all, not even for a second, and he was never a millionaire, although she kept implying it.

"Do you have a place I can crash at"?? N asked boldly.

"I have a place, but I'm sorry, you can't crash there. I've been down this road. I enjoyed it, but I can't go back there". The Ontario Street Original said, but he hadn't seen the turkey that was in the oven yet, not yet, and once again his big fuckin mouth was getting him in hot water without even noticing the steam.

She had French braids, white punk rocker/alternative typical.

Then there was a silver flash and they were talking to each other in Somerset Park late at night after "N" had gone to a liquor store. It was evilishly dark. Cops coming, time to split. No money for fines.

Then one day he was eating in a Chinese Restaurant and he saw her through a window on the back of a motor cycle. There was an Asian guy driving.

Silver again, and he was up very early, earlier than usual looking for a place to score breakfast and she was standing there wearing a cheap fur coat and a mini-skirt. They talked, verbally shot the shit and then parted ways after a quick hug.

Finally, one more flash of the silver kind.

His nerves had been wicked that morning, stuttering leaps in his stomach as he tried to get out of bed. He showered then, and headed for his usual eating spot on Somerset and instead found her with bare feet, crying, homeless, and once again they were going to kill her little dog if she didn't have a place for him to stay, he'd been abandoned to many times she said, that, and she couldn't provide them with a fixed address because she had none.

Dane had caved, he would take the little dog for a few days. He would feed it, walk it and what not. So he gave her his address so she could come and claim him sometime soon. Then she had gotten mad and said-"You can take him but you can't take me".

"I explained things to you". He said, and right as rain, he had. The Vultures were beginning to circle and swoop, only he still didn't notice. The radio station still wasn't coming in clear enough.

She had an agenda, one hell of a sinister bag of candy in mind . . . . Bitch!!!

They parted ways until they were supposed to meet and where she would turn over the dog. Still, he should've fuckin known better, it was going to lead to the downfall of everything.

Then when he encountered "N" she had her boyfriend with her, Chris. No problem, Dane had never developed any type of crush on this soon to be liability. He was introduced to Chris and the two strange bed fellows made fast friends.

"See, this is what I can do without". The bare chested street hanger said as "N" was busy yelling like a fuckin maniac at a landlord who apparently she claimed had beat her up. Her face was blood red with flush.

"I'd rather just sit underneath a tree and read". Chris said proudly displaying a folded paperback as he relaxed on a grassy knoll next to a seated Dane. "Yeah, I see what you mean". And he was about to rethink the prospect of taking in the dog who was running around he and Chris. It meant a connection to her, and that connection could mean serious trouble.

This stupid air head couldn't stay out of trouble or off of CRACK for even five minutes and for Christ sakes now she was flagging down a fuckin Police Cruiser. Dane was so mad that he felt like screaming.

He should leave her to her own devices, but he didn't. He got her out of it. Stuck up for her so that the cop wouldn't drag her off to jail and Sargent Kick Ass was not the least bit happy, and quite frankly, Dane could hardly blame him for his palpable anger.

Then after the cop was gone a strange fuckin thing happened. "N" dragged Dane and Chris down the street a ways where Dane broke off the engagement. He was not going to take the dog in after all.

"THAT'S GONNA COST YOU"!!! "N" screamed right in his face, the second such remark that day, the first was again over his not agreeing to lodge her along with the pooch.

"Now, that sounds like a threat". Chris warned her, equally as fused at her as Dane was.

Then things simmered down at Chris's tongue, and then "N" asked Dane to walk up the street with her so she could ask the woman in the restaurant for a glass of water, and then things got bizarre, because as "N" went inside Sargent Kick Ass rolled up in his cruiser with the pedal to the medal again.

What the fuck??

And this just minutes before Dane was going to politely dismiss himself and avoid this nuisance forever. He had NO USE for this HEAT SCORE!!! (Person who draws Police unnecessarily).

Now, Sargent Kick Ass wanted to know everything about Dane and how the fuck he knew "N".

Man, was Dane steamed. He spoke to the cop, telling the cop whatever he wanted to know as the cop fed everything back to him at a decibel that Dane was absolutely certain was audible to "N" even through the window.

What was this??

Something up.

When "N" came out the cop watched her ascend to the top of the street with Dane who was doing everything he could not to lose it, but he didn't.

"N" then made some remark about where Dane lived, in which building, and then she touched the roof of her mouth with the tip of her tongue and her eyes lit up with what Dane could best describe as DOLLAR SIGNS!!!

The turkey was finally sitting on the table in plain view. He knew the expression from Jimmy Shaker in Ransom when Tom Mullen told him that he would have paid ten times as much if he'd had any inclination that The Kidnappers would have honored their contract.

She was trying to establish an association.

Now, finally, Dane, like an idiot who had been asleep, was finally waking up.

Don't you get it asshole?? He was saying to himself.

She believed that he was loaded and flat out fuckin refused to be talked out of it. Now he got it, all of it, finally the total picture. Then he flashed on the image of her the night they met, the night he had first seen the bruises. She had never established who her attacker was with The Cops.

He hugged her and said goodnight as if nothing was wrong although everything was wrong and now he knew it.

Dane and "N" never saw nor spoke to one another ever again and he had returned home to Montreal.

There had been other times during that era that came and went. He had been frightened much of the time, and at some point, sitting in a steaming bath tub full of hot water he wondered why God had chosen to keep him on this earth when nothing seemed right. It had truly become a thing of nightmarish proportion where people who took advantage of The Phobic were in plentiful form.

In and out of malls, strip clubs, restaurants and dingy urban areas that he had known years ago. He had by one street girl that he didn't know been called a Merry Go Round, a term that in all his years on the street, Dane had never heard.

"What the fuck does that mean"?? He had asked her.

She explained that it meant someone who visually looks at girls for the sake of gratification, except that she had used more general terms.

"Is that your way of breaking the ice"?? He had asked, and then a day or two later she had smiled him an apology and always waved after that. Jesus Christ, this was a tough crowd, not like Montreal where they loved him right away. You had to fuckin work this crowd.

He had mad history in this city, years ago before ever meeting Lilly.

As he walked down Gladstone one night he remembered one of the best blow jobs that he'd ever gotten from a street hooker in 1997. It was definitely the blow job of that particular year. He had been alone one Saturday afternoon and decided to pick up a cute blond with an obvious breast augmentation who had at one time been a dancer. She had been nice to him, invited him back to wherever she was staying and took her top off. While she was rubbing his thigh and sucking his dick her two house mates, a busty black chick and a guy had descended the stairs dry sniffing as if they'd just done a couple of lines.

"OOPS, Sorry". The black chick had apologized.

"Hey, you guys are supposed to stay upstairs". The blond street hooker said smiling. "He has a nice body". She said rubbing his bare chest below his black and white NIKE track jacket that she had fully unzipped for him. She was making trails between his naval and his cock with her tongue at the same time.

It was one of those sexual experiences that you remembered as much for the ambiance as you did for the experience itself. There was just something about sitting on that sofa below those stairs in the shadows and having them walk in on them that was a turn on.

The blond with the hard, firm tits had been mesmerizing like nothing and no one that he had ever met, genuinely sweet, and not one bit put on. There was a legitimate warmth in her demeanour that seemed to crave the same.

The only regret that Dane had was not having fucked her, and now the thought turned him on like crazy. It was also the time, long before all of this other shit that had come to ruin his life that made him even harder when he remembered that experience.

He also loved the way that she had looked in her tight jeans with no top on. She had a tan as well although out of season, and she smelled like coconuts. She had even cuddled with him for about twenty minutes after he came.

If today Dane had a preference in women, it was street hookers. They were always kinder to him and treated him with far more respect than the average female of the nine to five variety.

Then there had been another morning at Somerset and Wellington when Dane had gotten between a former soldier, military cadet, or who knew fucking what of that variety who had wrestled a street hooker to the ground on the stairs of her building. He had her by the ankle when Dane had come along and hauled him off of her, pimply faced kid with a hard on.

"That's so sweet of you. Thank you". She had said right after, and then she'd begged him to come upstairs and cuddle with her … … … … Hold her for a while. As she'd put it.

That's why Dane preferred street hookers. They weren't afraid to get to know men, and were usually a lot more fun to be around, and like this one, many of them were former dancers so they looked damn good.

Now, in 2015, life was far more stressful and didn't share the same perks as years gone by. There was no devotion to being anything but fuckin phony and pretentious, then we had adopted this fixation on a disease called Political Correctness. Where had that come from??

There was nothing "NICE" about life anymore. We lived to feed ourselves and each other as much misery as we could handle. What had happened??

Like a friend of Danes whose Father was a Mafia Legend had said- "We're not ascending, we're spiraling down the fuckin toilet", and Dane had agreed, indeed we were. We had fed ourselves so much shit that it was coming out of our ears.

How had life that was at least one time pleasurable become an evil, half lit nightmare full of fear and dread??

Dane had no answer for that.

"You have to give them everything". Von "The Icon" said stepping out of the shower with his hair hanging from his head in wet lengthy strands.

"Give who everything"?? Andrew asked already half an hour late for a meeting with a high profile client.

"Your readers, you have to give them everything".

"I guess that's true. Look, I've gotta go, or I won't have a job. Kate made you a Lasagna, it's sitting on the bottom shelf of the fridge". Andrew said reaching below the overhang of the couch to grab his briefcase.

"Have fun". The Immortal Legend said heading into the bedroom to shed his bathrobe and change into his street clothes.

As he headed for his closet he began to remember the interview that he'd had to get the apartment where he and Ray had lived together.

The "Slum Lord", or land lord as this particular individual liked to fancy himself, had sat in front of Von who at the time was still a teenager and asked ... ... "Are you a fucking asshole"?? To which he had replied no, then "A" had handed over the keys. It was the easiest interview that Von had ever been the subject of.

Unfortunately, it had been "A" who had turned out to be a "Fucking asshole" after Von had put "A's" lowlife scumbag son in check one night outside the building. Then, things had changed. There were no more lovers over the town after that. Things in the building had gotten cold very fast, particularly in the rental office.

"I mean the fucking attitude"!! "A" had screamed slamming his fist down on top of the desk as what little wavy black head of locks that he had left fanned out behind him making him appear older than his fifty years.

"Uh-huh". Von had replied.

Then "A" threatened to take one of the guns that everyone knew that he owned and kill a mildly humoured Von "The Icon" who was not yet Von "The Icon".

To this day Von could not recall how that fucking exchange between two fucking assholes had ended.

Later, the quote "Bitch from Montreal", had come to see "A" while Dane was in the lobby of the building and fired him.

That was in 1994.

That was after, well, a bit after Dane had lived in Vancouver with the gorgeous, sweet, beautiful and talented Fiona MCAlister from Melbourne Australia who had turned out to be one of Danes favourite people in the entire world. He would gladly have married her had she not been previously engaged to Robert, whatever his name was back in Australia.

At the time Dane was working as a Security Officer for Woodwards Parkade in Gas Town which sat at the foot of the infamous East Hastings, the worlds largest open air market for narcotics, prostitution, and every other order of self destruction and/or addiction that existed.

He had also worked The Black Hills of East Hastings along the roads that were bordered with high grass and littered with needles, condoms, garros left behind by users too lazy to clean up after themselves etc.

Well, he was working that location for a company that had the contract. They had, had a rash of automobile break ins who were mostly I.V. Drug Users looking to get their hands on something they could hawk to make a quick buck or sell to a pedestrian on the sidewalk who was desperate enough to buy their product.

Dane had caught one such addict breaking into an all terrain vehicle with a crowbar in his knap sack. When the subject had refused to relinquish what was in the sack Dane had hit him in the head with a left hook and dropped him to the floor of the garage, and what a shit storm that had turned out to be on Monday morning. And Dane was violent and out of control and should not have done something so maniac ... ... ish, to which Dane had replied ... ... "Uh-huh"!!!

Then someone had reported that Dane had shown up to work dressed like a Pre-Eminem era Rapper decked out in green hang downs, a Raiders jacket, and a ball cap twisted backwards. This was genuinely one of the largest insults that David Dane had ever received. He would not have been caught dead at his own funeral wearing such apparel. Ridiculous!!!

Then, there had come the final straw following Danes alleged outburst at a subject of a call at an apartment complex on Bidwell, which for Danes career as a Security Officer, should have been called "Farewell".

It was during a fireworks display on Canada day that Dane had been taken to task by an affluent looking Arabic gentlemen who didn't like being told that he had to wait in line to get into the building like everyone else, and Dane was a punk, and this may very well be the last time that Dane ever worked in this town. He had been right about the last part.

Things had degenerated, quickly, and Dane and the Arabic gentleman with the solid looking arms and the epic blond on his arm were soon eyeball to eyeball in a stare down/standoff.

It had been The Arabs lucky day, because Dane had not decided to kill him and make him look like a "Fucking Asshole" just for starting the whole thing to begin with. Arrogant bastard.

They continued to butt noses in the reflection of the fireworks which were shining in the windows.

Dane said this, Captain Cock Sucker said that, and eventually the sonovabitch had turned and left uttering a slew of profanities that would make a soldier blush.

Then Monday morning came again, and Dane shouldn't have done something so maniac … … ish and his conduct was not becoming of a team player at (Name Omitted), Security. Then there were outrageous allegations-Dane had strong armed the subject, he had used profanities, he had uttered death threats which Dane would hear of himself doing at least once more in his life, yada, yada, yada. To which Dane replied … … … … … "Uh-huh"!!!

Then came the two dreaded words from the mouth of his tyrannical boss who should have quote "Never given someone like him a uniform in the first place". To which Dane had replied … … … … … "You are a fucking asshole"!!!

However, while the job had lasted, it had afforded Dane some highly interesting experiences that he would write about somewhere, someday. One such experience had involved a writer who had come to Montreal to publish his manuscript using all of his savings to get there, and then suffering the loss of his life.

The poor sonovabitch had parked on one of the levels at Woodwards to go and get a bite to eat in Gas Town, and when he had returned he had found his automobile broken into and his duffel bag, which contained the only copy of the manuscript, gone!!!

His wife was also present.

Dane had never been so sympathetic to a client, or subject of a call so to speak in his entire six month career as a Security Officer, however short lived.

Still to this day, he could remember specifically telling the guy that he too was a writer, so he easily understood his suffering. When you wrote a book it was the same as giving birth to a child and raising it, and the thought of someone stealing it was akin to a sub human act. These motherfuckers should have been executed!!!

It was about a half an hour later with the description of the duffel bag that Dane looked over into Blood Alley which ran between the two buildings and spotted a guy carrying the green duffel bag.

"HEY"!!! He had yelled running down one of the ramps toward the door that led to the alleyway and tossing it open.

"Hey loser"!!! Dane had called out approaching the nervous looking thief who wore a bandana. But it was bad timing, standing there in a panel of sun light between those two stretches of parking lot, because as Dane approached the guy face on, someone else called out to him in general language. When Dane turned to see who it was he got a heavy fist in the mouth that drew a lot of blood.

Sadly, the guy with the car, who had spent all of his savings to get to Vancouver, never saw his book again, and to this day, Dane felt responsible.

There was also the time that Dane had gotten in the middle of two bare chested, toothless natives who were fighting over a remarkably ugly woman near the foot of the black hills. Everything had come off, watches, shirts, even shoes had been lost, and now Dane was swinging along with them.

The fight had ended when Dane had cleared out the first row of teeth of the guy who had most likely been the instigator.

"You fuckin bastard"!!! The guy had yelled.

"You won't be able to say that tomorrow morning". Dane had retorted.

Another experience had seen Dane chase a female street hooker into The Sunrise Hotel which was infamous along East Hastings seedy upper strip. When Dane had gotten to her room she had taken everything off amidst a pool full of needles in the middle of the floor and begged Dane to fuck her instead of arresting her. It hadn't worked, and her clothes, as well as a pair of hand cuffs had ended up on her instead.

Dane had never forgotten the smell of decay or that of defecation in that room. It had been horrible.

Many of those girls had lived like animals back then, the conditions were evil, and Dane had known some of them, particularly memorable were the ones that Pig Farmer/Serial Killer Robert William Pickton had killed.

When the case had gone to trial Dane had picked up a newspaper and scanned some of the faces, many of them were familiar, some were friends that he knew from along the stroll or The Black Hills. As far as Dane was concerned, they should have hanged Willy Pickton.

One time a female Street Hooker friend of Danes that Dane couldn't resist had invited him back to her room on a Sunday evening. She had stripped down to her bra and panties and asked Dane to lay back on the bed.

As Dane had looked over at the window he took stalk of the security measures that these women took to protect themselves. There was a bar of wood with nails driven through it lying below the reach of the window pane so that should one attempt entry, their hands would end up looking as Christs did on the cross.

"It gets scary living up here". She had said to him as she unfastened his jeans.

"Yeah, it certainly looks that way doesn't it". He had responded also noticing the bed that they were stretched out on. It was a box spring mattress held together by two large brown wooden arches with three or four pillars running to each of its lengths. It looked like something that belonged back in WW2.

Dane would never, ever forget that room, nor the sexy little Goddess who had been such a good friend over time. She was awesome, and to this day, Dane prayed that Robert Pickton had never gotten to her as he had so many of his other friends. Cock Sucker!!!

East Hastings at eighteen years of age had been one of the most haunting memories of David Danes life, it was in a way, part of what had prepared him for Lilly Chicoine.

One night after work Dane had met a guy named Todd who gave Dane a brief introduction to The Rave scene in East Hastings.

The place had been bathed in blood red light awash in full over a crowd of I.V. Drug users who didn't seem the least bit shy about displaying their habits for anyone who came through the door. There were syringes passing from one to another in plain view, a bevy of AIDS prospects.

Then there was a place within, known as "The Caverns". It was a series of adjoined Hallways where you could invariably pick your poison or fix. Drugs were being sold at tables as baseball cards were at the Flee Market. There was BLACK TAR HEROIN, LIFE, SMACK, and even a brand known on the street as NINJA TURTLE.

Aside from that there was a supermarket of pills, pipes, this, that and the other. Dane thought it was a wonder that The Police didn't bother to raid the place in full combat gear. How the fuck did they manage to get away with this??

As Dane and Todd passed through a series of doors Dane took stock of the general attire worn by most of the RAVERS. It was cabaret style, or a sort of "GAY BIKER" look, plenty of leather chaps and leather straps worn below Biker Caps of a variety that Dane had seen in Biker apparel stores over the years.

When they were through touring the inner core of the building Todd took Dane up onto the roof which overlooked Main and Hastings, or, Pain and Wastings, and fired up a cigarette.

"Welcome to Hell". He said, to which Dane had nodded in response.

When Dane had returned home later that night he had found Fiona sound asleep in her bedroom with the door open. He longed to go in and hold her in his arms. He was madly in love with her although she probably hadn't realized it yet.

Christ, she was beautiful, and her room always smelled of perfumes and roses. He was crazy about her. She would come to realize this later, but not yet.

Fiona- I know that you'll probably never get to read this because you're long gone from my life. I just want you to know that you were one of the sweetest, kindest, most genuinely beautiful people that I've ever known. I love you angel, wherever you are or whoever you ended up with. I want you to know that saying that you're special just isn't enough.

I remember you one time mentioning that you were a quote "Damn good friend", but the truth is that you sold yourself short. You're the best friend anyone could ever ask for, and your track record speaks for itself. I CANNOT say enough positive things to do you justice.

I love you at this moment, and forever Goddess.

As you would have ended,
Cheers

One night while working The Black Hills Dane had met a street girl who had taken him back to her house which literally looked like it had been born up and out of Hell sitting in the midst of tall grass with most of the paint chipped off of it. The place was genuinely eerie and Dane wondered who was paying the hydro bill. There were lights, bright fucking yellow which he had never forgotten.

Then she had pulled out a wooden box from underneath a table and offered him a syringe to which he had winced, and the hooker sitting by the lamp had blood on her hands. She was dressed in white from head to toe.

Dane had decided to leave unexpectedly, and his hostess hadn't looked impressed. It was late and he was horny, otherwise he wouldn't have come here at all. Talk about giving you the creeps.

"Bad, bad". He had uttered below his breath as he'd made his way back out onto the sidewalk which was littered with condoms, syringes, Trojan wrappers, garros, fresh trash, and just about anything and everything else that one could think of.

He had then ventured into a local strip club where there was a floor show under way, literally. The Stripper was dancing amidst a group of guys who had placed their chairs around her in a circle in place of a stage. She was fingering herself and screaming "I'M CUMMING"!!! At the top of her lungs.

And now he wanted to fuck her, bad.

"How much do you have"?? The Dancer had asked when she was finished her set.

After accepting the Brownie that Dane handed her she took him into the shadows near a back door and fucked him like tomorrow wasn't on the horizon. She had mesmerized him.

All his life, well, at least all his life that existed after fifteen years of age Dane had always been attracted to the under belly of society, it held a certain mystique in his eyes.

And Fiona had always been there late, after he'd gotten home, pure class and no underbelly to speak of. She belonged to the opposite. If there was a living angel, then it was Fiona. To this day he loved her far beyond words. Sweetness and light brought to life. What a genuinely terrific and special human being.

If the words-"One of a kind" were created to fit one soul like a glass slipper, then that one person was Fiona MCAlister.

If Dane had a million dollars today he would have gladly traded it to have Fiona back in his life.

After Fiona had left to head back overseas, Chris Markem had moved in with David Dane. In many ways Markem had mentored Dane in ways that were still apparent today. He had taught Dane how to Box as well as how to be a Bad Ass. The two also shared the same voracious appetite for exotic dancers, street girls, and bad women in general. There was something about a bad ass that made the heart beat faster.

One day, after several hours of drinking, Chris had invited a homeless wino home to drink with him because Dane did not himself drink alcohol. At around seven or eight thirty that night, and after listening to this particular drunken lunatic rant about God and Jesus, The Bible, Oprah Winfrey, homosexual racoons and whatever else, Chris Markem finally looked quizzically across the room at Dane and asked him-"You know why I brought Bill home to drink with us"??

"I don't have a clue". Dane had responded.

"Well you see how he goes on"?? Markem asked. "Well that's how you go on". He answered sitting back to the wall wearing a blazer and blue jeans, one ankle crossed over the other with a bottle of Rum between his legs.

Dane had never laughed so hard in his life.

"That's what I have to live with". The uncommonly good looking Markem said standing up and heading for the bathroom to take a piss.

There was no Fighter/Comedian like him.

Markem would regularly boast ... ... "Women tend to be very sexually concerned with me David".

One night, Dane told him that, that was because he rarely used protection.

One night after leaving a Billiards Club Dane had watched Markem beat the living Swarma out of six Iranians who had decided to accost him as he put his blazer over his shoulders.

Chris Markems common pick up line in a club was ... ... "Hi, my name's Chris, wanna fuck me"?? And more times than not he had gotten a yes.

Jesus Christ, more and more trips all the way down memory lane.

He was a good fighter, dangerous, and if you fucked with Chris Markem you were probably at the very least going to the hospital. Fight was something that the males, and even some of the females in The Markem Family knew how to do and do well, a born science.

Back home in Nova Scotia, Dane, a guy named Randy, and a Hispanic Gigolo named Moises had met Chris Markem while he was working at the local Y as a trainer. They had immediately hated him, and once told an African American Body Builder who trained there that they were going to beat the shit out of Chris and not spare the horses. It was then that they were informed that Markem was a seasoned Boxer who had two times won The Alberta Championship and was also, formerly, a Greco Roman Wrestling titlist. That had changed everything.

"Yeah, and don't fuckin stare at me across the room either". Markem had once warned them.

Later, on, after Randy had violently turned against Dane, it was Chris Markem who came to Danes aid and offered to train him. Markem couldn't stand The Czech punk who thought he was hot shit and deserved to be put in his place.

Dane had spent Christmas Day and Night 1993 with The extremely dangerous and revered Markems. They, particularly he and Jack, were born and bred to look like Porn Star/Street Fighters out of a movie. Jack who was the younger, and closest Brother of Chris, was also a touted bad ass, thug and street fighter who had a softer side for those that he liked. He resembled Chris, although Jack had a moustache, and a different demeanour.

Dane to this day was proud of his association with The Markems, and still boasted of it whenever he was around those who knew them.

Robert and Richard, who were friends of The Markems had also mentored David Dane. They were affectionately known as "The Brothers From The Ghetto" and if there was a single soul on this planet who didn't fucking love them, then Dane did not know who that soul was. Robert and Richard were, at least as far as Dane was concerned, the greatest credit to their race who had ever lived. If any two human beings deserved to represent The African American/ African Canadian race then it was Richard and Robert. They were simply the absolute highest caliber individuals that their race had to offer. There were none like them.

One funny story that took place was on a Wednesday afternoon when one of Danes friends who didn't normally go to the gym had accompanied him, and upon seeing Richard and Robert, he had asked. "Are they related"??

Dane couldn't believe it. "No you fuckin idiot, they're identical strangers". He had responded.

When Dane had told this story to Chris later on he had characterized Danes friend as a quote "Fuckin mutant, idiot, dummy"!!!

Had it not been for Chris and Jack, Robert and Richard, Dane would not, could not, be the man that he was today. All four men had given him what he needed to be who he was, particularly Chris Markem.

They had helped to prepare him in the realms of Body Building, Boxing, and the street. That, and the legendary Chris Markem had taught Dane everything that he knew about style and panache, which was considerable. Markem at his highest peaks was a superstar whom few others could equal.

Robert and Richard exemplified each and every single thing that the term "ROLE MODEL" was meant to imply and lived up to it to the mark in their day to day lives. There wasn't a soul on this earth who didn't respect them and hold them in the highest regard.

Jack was good at being quietly dangerous. He didn't have to say much to intimidate the most sinister of opponents in the street. Dane had once characterized him as having a murderous air about him.

On Christmas Day 93 Chris Markem had proved one thing in spades to a young David Dane. There was "AB-SO-LUTELY, NO ONE" on this planet who could match him for looks, style, and charisma. Had there been a title, then Markem would've been the champion. He had at the time been seventeen years older than Dane, and there was nothing that Dane could have done on any level to compete with him.

Nothing!!!

Dane still recalled Chris standing up with his glass, earring shimmering in the light, toasting everyone in the room. He was better looking than ten movie stars. A born leader who had "HIGH END BOXING TITLIST" tattooed on the very surface of his appearance.

Chris had coached Dane in sub zero temperatures behind his Mother house in Spryfield on a bag that hung from a back porch often teaching him to run drills, duck walk, push the pavement on the driveway, and shadow box.

"We'll train you real proper like". Chris had told Dane in his Newfoundland accent. In that domain, Markem had honored his word to the bone.

"How'd you get out here for your lesson today"?? Markem had once asked Dane.

"I took the bus".

"Why not let the bus take you"?? His Coach had responded in his typical dry wit.

"That's good. That's very good". Dane had said dryly trying to offset his trainers wit.

Chris would also typically boast that he quote "Tended to be slightly more erotic than David Dane".

"This is my orgasmic sweater". He would tell him.

"Orgasmic"?? Dane had once asked with a quizzically raised eye brow.

"Women touch this sweater and then they lose control of themselves". Markem replied grabbing a thumb and forefinger worth of his shirt and making a quick, mock woman having an orgasm sound. "I can't take this shirt to the dry cleaners like". Markem commented.

When Dane awoke from his day dream he was splayed out on his Brothers couch in the living room, still wearing his white bathrobe that he had on from earlier that morning.

Jesus, what time was it?? Dane wondered getting up from his seated position and looking at the digital display on the cable converter box.

"Seven forty five". He said slipping his watch over his wrist and heading for the shower.

CHAPTER V

When Von awoke the following morning there was a knock on the door. "Aww … … … … Jesus Christ". He complained, dragging himself away from the current of sleep. "Who is it"?? He asked fishing around the chair for his jeans that were buried beneath a heap of laundry.

"It's who it's not, it's not Publishers Clearing House, you have not won a million dollars". Ray said walking past Von as he opened the door. Von had opened the door, Ray had walked through it.

"Roof"!!! WARRIOR barked jumping down off of the bed and heading into the living room to join his owner and his former flat mate. Vons former flat mate. WARRIOR had never signed a lease in his life.

"Good morning to you to". Von said pulling a shirt out of the chair, yes chair.

"Listen, there is a very big problem". Ray said.

"Yeah, I can see that, otherwise you wouldn't be here at half past seven fuckin a.m.".

"I spoke to your friends. They want to meet with you face to face".

"Did you tell them that if they don't back the fuck off their business is gonna be all over the nine o' clock news"??

"It doesn't matter. They want to see you anyway".

"Well, at least they're not tired of my presence". Dane remarked.

"What do you want me to tell them"?? The Sweet Black Man asked removing his three quarter length black leather jacket and tossing it over the nape of the couch.

"I'm not walking into a firefight with these people. Don't go near them with anything less than a Bazooka".

"Can I have one of those"?? Ray asked pointing to a box of waffles that Andrew had left aboard the counter.

"You can have the entire fuckin box for all I care".

"And there's one other incentive". Ray explained.

"Uh-huh"??

"They have your Mother". He said.

"Excuse me, how's that"??

"They have your Mother. She is not in a coma anymore".

Vons face had turned from white to an off shade of grey. "Just a minute, I need to call the hospital". The Boxer said reaching into the pocket of his leather jacket. As soon as he had located what he had been looking for he began dialling.

"Hello, Montreal General". The Switch Board Operator responded.

"Yeah, I'm looking for an I.C.U. patient Von explained. "Her name's Marilyn Dane". He said spelling out the last name upon request. "WHEN"?? He hollered hearing the switch board operators response.

"She was discharged four weeks ago". The Operator explained.

"Oh, fuckin Jesus". Ray yelled having heard the response over the phone.

"What the fuck do they want?? I don't get it?? This isn't gonna buy them Jack Shit"!!!

"They want you to be there. They are going to speak to us".

"Nah, there's something else going on here. We're gonna end up walking nose first into some variety of ambush with "JACK ASS" tattooed on our foreheads.

"Maybe they're just mad at you". Ray proclaimed.

"Like that's any better. I hate to say this, but I wish that Jenny had never brought these people to my door"

"She did. Now you have to deal with it".

WARRIOR was sniffing Rays jeans now.

"We're gonna need fire power". Dane said in a serious(This is as grave as it gets-tone of voice).

"Guns".

"Yup, and on short notice".

"I know some Crips". Ray offered straight faced.

"Call your friends. Tell them that we need heavy artillery, Uzi's or some shit".

"We are going to fuckin jail".

"Jail's better than the grave yard. I'd rather be tried by twelve than carried by six". VON said borrowing a line from the late Norm Meekison.

"I'll see what I can do". Ray said.

That night Von and Ray waited in the silent darkness in the park on St. Alexandre De Seve for the representatives of the shadowy group that had requested their presence. They were supposed to be here at nine p.m., not a moment later, yet nine p.m. came and went, and still there was no sound but the rustling of the leaves from the tree tops, and no presence but that of themselves.

Sharp whisps of silver light bled through the cracks in the greenery as they waited.

"Where the fuck are these jack rabbit … … … … … Von asked, voicing his frame of mind.

Ray was shaking his head now. "I don't fuckin understand". He said.

Then, at nine fifteen Von and Ray got the surprise of a lifetime, when a roughed up, torn clothed Marilyn Dane stumbled over the sloped foot path walking in their direction. Her Mascara had run and her lip stick was smeared across her left cheek.

"Mum"!!! Von called out rushing to embrace his Mother who collapsed into his arms crying.

Von and Ray were looking at each other now, completely bewildered. None of this made a stitch of sense.

"I don't fuckin get it". Ray said in a low, gravelly voice that didn't seem to belong to him.

"What the hell happened"?? Dane asked his Mother who wore a white sweater with a flower design made from sequins over white casual pants. Both items of clothing were spattered with blood that was soaked through to the flesh.

Von and Rays voices both seemed to echo backward from someplace else, it was as if their words weren't their own but were instead somehow pre-recorded to fit with this funereal sequence of events.

Marilyn released her sons embrace and then walked away from him.

Something here didn't seem to belong to the waking world. Von registered, conscious of the firearm that was tucked below his waist band. He simply could not believe his eyes, nor anything else that was transpiring around him.

Rays mind was swimming, doing laps around itself.

"Talk to me". Von ordered his Mother, but she gave no response, leaving her back turned.

Leaves rustling in the wind and shards of moonlight seeping through the cracks in the lattice work.

"What did they do to you"?? Von asked, again speaking to her back.

"Where's Andrew"?? He whispered to Ray who was taking all of this in.

"I don't know". He said.

"Let's get her home". Von reconciled.

"If I had been half, half the person that you're saying I am I would've gone to jail years ago"!!! Eddy professed looking across the room at the blond that he had been dating for six months. "It's not like you couldn't have accepted my offer to get off of this gravy train when I showed you the door". The Wrestler said firing a crystal tumbler against the wall and watching it shatter.

"You bastard" Melina yelled bursting into a rage. "I stayed with you because I loved you, even when you were out screwing every ring rat that moved"!!! The erotic looking twenty five year old former porn starlet yelled.

"Yeah, like you had any better offers". Eddy retorted gyrating his hips in fashion of his character. "I could've fucked anyone, your old lady if I'd wanted to, but the goddamn line was to long".

"Yeah", she hollered twisting around on the couch. "Wouldn't it be just like you to try and do something like that"??

"Yeah, it would, so you better pray to holy hell that I don't decide to do it. I could have done that on our second date".

"FUCK YOU, YOU FUCKIN COCK SUCKER!!! MAYBE I SHOULD GO FUCK YOUR AUTHOR FRIEND"!!!

"What the hell did you just say to me"?? Eddy shouted making a Bee line for her.

"This is fuckin alcoholism talking. You need to get help for your problem"!!!

"They don't have rehab to help you deal with whores". Eddy said giving her slow chase around the edge of the couch. He was sick of this bitches bold, brazen mouth.

"Yeah, that's it Eddy, beat me up, oh big man"!!! She taunted as Eddy slowed down still with it enough somewhere to know that he shouldn't go any further with what he was doing.

"BASTARD"!!! She screamed tossing a stiletto in his general direction.

"Ye know, you're so fuckin sick that it turns my insides. You wanna repeat that part about screwing Von"!!!

"I'll give him the best fuckin head of his life"!!! Melina threatened.

"I'll kill you you bitch"!!! Eddy threatened coming after her this time as she backed off and ran for the phone.

"WHO THE FUCK ARE YOU GONNA CALL BITCH"??? Eddy hollered lunging for her dress as she screamed heading toward the phone.

"Yeah, 911. My name is … … … … … … … …

"Put the phone DOWN"!!! Eddy hollered in the back ground.

"Mam, please stay on the line with us. We have a patrol car en-route Just stay calm".

"I SAID PUT IT DOWN"!!!! Eddy hollered seething like a mad man, his white dress shirt was unbuttoned to the middle of his chest, his shirt that he had worn above white dress pants to give a speech to a group of women tonight. Eddy Dorozowsky was a corporate sponsor albeit his wrestling image as a playboy.

"AGHE" … … … … … Melina screamed as Eddy grabbed the phone from her and tossed it against the wall.

He was slowly advancing upon her now, the alcohol having its way. He had drank casually before the presentation, and heavily afterwards. It was showing now, his eyes were blood shot and his pupils dilated.

"You should've fucked my Mother cause she would've busted your balls"!!! Melina hollered.

"Then maybe I … … … … … … … …

"Open the door … … … … … POLICE"!!! A voice echoed from the other side.

"Tell them that I left". Eddy said grabbing a set of car keys from a crystal table that stood to the side of the couples lavish living room that PRO WRESTLING had paid for. There were tokens of his career everywhere, even framed magazine covers. He had appeared on the front page of WRESTLING TODAY at least eight times.

"Where is he"?? The younger of the two male Police officers asked through the door.

"He just left". Melina said collapsing into the first of the two officers arms.

"Are you alright"?? Officer Cambridge asked as the sound of squealing tires made its way around the side of the house, burning rubber.

"Shit, call it in". Officer Blane Williams ordered. "What's his plate number"?? Russ Cambridge asked.

"XXX EDDY"!!! Melina divulged crumbling to her knees. "It's one of those personalized plates. He thinks he's Gods gift". She said the bottom of her silk blue gown fanning out around her knees.

Williams called it in, non plussed. They'd been out here twice this month already and still her hot head lover wouldn't wise up.

"Okay, was he drinking tonight"?? Cambridge asked through a thick French drawl.

"Yeah … … … … … … … yes". Melina said nodding from her position on her knees. "He's violent when he drinks".

"Okay, did he hit you tonight?? Did he strike you"?? Williams questioned.

Melina again responded by shaking her head, this time it was NO!!!

"Okay, we're gonna talk to him".

"Talk to him. That's all that you ever do is talk to him"!!! She yelled.

"Okay, mam. We're the Police. We're gonna decide what happens, not you".

Again, The Police were sucking Eddys ass because he was a celebrity.

Around the corner and two blocks over from the house the celebrity Pro Wrestler known as Triple XXX SEXXXY EDDY was fishing around the glove compartment for one of his cell phones. The hour was late, past eleven, but if he did get arrested tonight he wanted to be sure that he had representation, and now she was threatening to suck Vons dick. She'd probably try to suck his lawyer as well.

If Eddy had his way he would dig this womans eyes out with a hunting knife. She knew who the fuck he was, and that he was the biggest star in Montreal history, bar none. She had been lucky that he'd ever picked her off of that bar stool at that after party. That, and had it not been for him she'd still be trying to hawk paintings on the boardwalk in Old Montreal during the summertime.

One way or another, and she wasn't going to fuckin haunt him. He would drop her like a hot potato in front of the world and maybe for one of her friends, maybe Rena with the huge jugs and then again who in Christs name was Von "The SO CALLED ICON" anyway??

"Yeah, Prescott, it's Eddy. I'm sitting around the corner in my car. I think The Police are going to arrest me tonight. I had an out with Melina. You need to call me as soon as you get this". Eddy said, and then dropped his digits.

It was raining now, silver drops falling in a light force in front of the grill.

So, she really wanted to suck Von that bad. She was a slut when he met her, working off and on doing porn shoots and just barely getting by on peanuts. He'd put her back where she came from, and all at once.

When Von and Ray got Marilyn back to Andrews condo it was obvious that she was all but despondent, shut down, and out of communicado with the outside world. Her mascara was run, but it had dried, as if she'd been crying for hours and hours but had at some point, stopped.

"Mum, you don't wanna talk"?? Andrew pressed her, but he got not a syllable, nothing.

"I think maybe we oughta call a doctor". The Legendary Von "The Icon" said.

"It is for sure that something is wrong". Ray echoed in his own words.

She was awake, however turned off to the outside world.

Just then Vons phone lit up. The call display read "Barclay".

"Yeah, someone wants you down here tomorrow night, kind of a surprise party".

"Where are you"?? Von asked turning around with a frown on his face.

"We're at The Domino old buddy. Just show up around nine. Someone wants to see you. He's bent hard".

"You're not gonna tell me who it is"?? Von asked beginning to seethe with anger at the prospect of being kept in the dark. He'd show up alright, and whoever this mystery person was they better bring a tire iron.

"Who the fuck was that"?? Ray asked.

"A friend of mine". The Icon said.

Von thought that was the strangest call that he'd ever gotten. He was the boss. Who was Barclay to tell him that he wasn't gonna tell him who the fuck it was who wanted to see him??

"Did you hook him"?? Scott Paris asked leaning over the back of a chair. He was dressed in a light blue denim vest over skin tight blue jeans tucked into a pair of black leather boots.

"Yeah, I hooked him alright". Barclay said, laughing.

The following night "The Immortal" Von "The Icon", the man who had proudly represented Ontario Street, been their hero and champion, and written two books about their neighbourhood, walked through the door to The Black Domino Tavern at nine p.m. to a round of applause.

"SURPRISE"!!! Barclay yelled, tossing his massive tattooed arms around his long time buddy and friend. "Good to see you". The big man said.

"Hey mano, this is your welcome back party". Paris said standing next to Troy.

"Surprise Uncle Von". Kate "The Gate" said appearing out of nowhere.

"Hey angel, how you doin"?? The Immortal one said embracing his niece.

Then a side door came open, and SEXXXY EDDY walked through it dressed in a white shirt and black pants. Von immediately thought that something was off, not sure what, fuse burning of some kind, nearing its wick. It was in his eyes and his demeanour. The radio station was still slightly out of tune, registering deceit, but with no catalyst.

This was typical self, picking up every trace of what went on in the room.

"Good to see you". Von said reaching out and shaking Eddys hand.

"What's up Von"?? Eddy asked squeezing his long time buddies hand, too hard.

Smile not right, over cooked. Von registered like a device designed to read signals. There was something in this fish tank that stunk.

"Should we cut the cake"?? Ray asked appearing from beneath the bar. He had been in on the surprise as well.

"Happy to have you back Mr. Magnum". Ray said extending a kind and genuine hand to his friend.

"Thanks Ray". The legendary Von "The Icon" said.

Eddy was moving around the room now, making rounds, he had a crowd to please, so many fans.

WARRIOR was also present, wearing a black bow tie and baring a sign around his thick neck which read-"WELCOME HOME DADDY"!!!

"Somebody cut him a piece of cake". Von said glancing in WARRIORS general direction.

"I wanna propose a toast". Eddy said raising a Champagne glass that was sparkling at the center with bubbly. "To an Immortal Legend". He said letting his smile fade on the final word.

"Thanks Eddy". Von said giving his friend a solid hand shake, yet at the same time noticing what was in Eddys eyes as his own expression hardened by reflex.

Just then Melina appeared out of nowhere and attempted to place herself between Von and her husband but Ontario Streets Immortal Icon paid her little mind glancing over her head with a steely look in his eyes. What the fuck was she trying to do??

"Please excuse me". Von said making a u turn around Melina and then disappearing into the crowd that had come to celebrate his home coming.

Later that night as Von stepped through the side door to get some air, he again encountered Melina who was wearing her best "COME HITHER" look. "Great party". She said attempting to close the distance between herself and her husbands friend.

Von was nodding calmly now, still sipping on his drink.

"You wanna have a second party tonight"?? Melina asked resting her palm on The Ontario Street Originals left pectoral.

"This isn't going anywhere". Von said stepping back. He wasn't about to do that to his friend, and at the same time he wondered what the fuck was in this womans head.

"You don't wanna go somewhere and take a shower with me"?? She asked pressing herself against him.

He was shaking his head now, eyes turned slightly upward. "Nope".

"You don't wanna have sex with … … … … … … … … … …

Just then Eddy appeared seemingly out of a cloth of shadows.

"Sorry, what was that last part"?? Eddy asked her with his face screwed up. He looked almost twisted, Von registered. "Did you just offer to sleep with Von"?? Eddy asked as The Ontario Street Original looked the other way. Right now, he wanted to be anywhere but here, even a holding cell would be more comfortable than this.

"Did I just hear you show my friend what a fuckin whore my wife really is"?? Eddy asked unleashing a verbal tirade. "You're a fuckin traitor. I should kill you just for making a statement like that"!!! Eddy threatened. "What did she offer to do for you"?? He demanded as a light rain began to fall.

"C mon Von, did she offer to suck you?? What"?? Eddy continued.

"I'm gonna leave you guys to it". Von said ready to turn and go back the way that he came.

"Nah, I wanna hear what she said first". Eddy said grabbing a handful of his friends shirt.

"Eddy, this is between you and your wife. Get your hand off me". Von warned with little conviction. He understood his friends pain. He had been in such situations himself.

Eddy had dropped his grip, but inside he wanted to kill his friend, for SEXXXY EDDY had enormous pride.

"If you ever touch my fuckin wife again, I'll kill you". Eddy said warningly.

"I never touched your wife. I'm going back inside". Von concluded.

"He wants me". Melina said glaring in Vons direction.

"No, I don't". Von said in a flat voice, and he meant it.

"You think there are no more surprises tonight". Eddy asked.

"Here's a little WELCOME BACK music". The Wrestler said flooring Von "The Icon" with an ominous kick to the side of the skull.

Just then Paris and Barclay appeared in the light at the side door way.

"Give em one more". Barclay said lifting Von by the chin and dropping him with a left hammer hook as he had self named the punch.

Paris was looking down at the fallen hero who was bleeding now. "Give Von "The Icon" one more for the road". Paris said as Kate Shamrock appeared out of nowhere and attacked him.

"You're supposed to be his friend"!!! The titlist shouted in Eddys direction.

"Whoaaaa"!!! Eddy said demonstrating his trademark gyration.

At that moment Ray came through the door swinging for all he was worth leveling Eddy with a left, right, left combination to the head.

Eddy then did a kip up, returning fire with a series of high kicks, one after another.

"C mon Scott, let's go". Kate taunted, although she knew she was way over matched.

Von was unconscious now, lying flat to one side of the melei. His eyes were closed on darkness.

"Whoooa"!!! Eddy said again field kicking Von "The Icon" in the gut.

Paris swung at Kate now, dispatching her assault with a single violent blow to the head. "Nighty, night Princess"!!! He said as Ray and Eddy squared off one on one. "C mon Wrestler". Ray said drawing a switch blade. He was out numbered three to one.

Just then Barclay grabbed Ray lifting him off his feet. He then jack knifed him back first into the pavement with a thud. "Yeah, that's the price of fame. There's a new name for my signature move Scott" Eddy said ripping his dress shirt off and pitching it in Vons face. "Welcome home old buddy". He said.

Melina was smiling now. Fuck him for rejecting her.

Eddy, Paris, and Barclay were now low fiving one another.

"This is "THE LIME LIGHT" Eddy hollered stand straddling "The Immortal" Von "The Icon" who was lying prone on his back.

"Where's the fuckin Barrister"?? Barclay asked laughing like a maniac.

"I think someone spiked his Orange Crush". Paris admitted.

As soon as everything was quiet, a tall, dark handsome playboy with a diamond stud in his left ear emerged from the shadows. "This is the final act David". Chris Markem said embracing Paris, Barclay, and Eddy, one after another.

"The Fourth Man is finally here". Scott Paris announced.

"You didn't see that comin did ye lad"?? Markem asked his fallen protégé. "Jackie and I talked about this for a long time". The Rico Suave Bad Boy said in reference to his younger Brother (Jack), whom he referred to as Jackie. It was something that had started when they were kids.

"Turn em over like". Markem said with a tooth pick perched between his curved lips. He had a mouth like Sylvester Stallone, and too many, there was a resemblance.

Because of his looks, he had once been nicknamed, HOLLYWOOD!!!

"Who's the real icon"?? He asked his unconscious protégé who was beginning to slowly come to.

"Put em out again". Markem ordered glaring down at his student as his massive brown eyes smouldered with incentive and something else. He looked intense. He had BAD ASS written all over him. To Dane, Chris Markem had always been an icon. Dane had patterned himself after the man who was now standing over him.

Scott Paris and Troy Barclay were clowning, each demonstrating a different over exaggerated muscular pose.

"I'll hold em up, and you hit em like". Markem directed SEXXXY EDDY who was tuning up the band with a series of stomps. "Get up"!!! The Legendary RICO SUAVE BAD BOY ordered lifting his protégés limp carcass to his feet. "Alright, hit em". Markem ordered as Eddy lifted his heel and back kicked his former friend in the mouth.

Von "The Icon" again crumpled to the ground, his face swollen beyond recognition.

"You're a product of me like David. You're stance should be more solid than that". The Icon said, cold as ice, adjusting his black silk Do Rag that he wore over a stubble beard, blazer, and faded blue jeans.

Markem was one of the few white males whom Dane had ever seen wear a Do Rag, but he had always managed to pull it off with extreme style and character. The look truly suited his square jaw and ring hardened features.

"Let's go". Markem ordered leading the three men to a black four door sedan that he had rented a day ago. "Dane won't forget this night anytime soon, will he"?? Markem asked turning to Eddy. "These streets belong to us now" ... ... He said. THE HOSTILE TAKE OVER, HAD BEGUN!!!!

One night later, before a gathered crowd of close to a thousand on Ontario Street, SEXXXY EDDY stood with Scott Paris and Troy Barclay to either shoulder. The entire world had heard about what had happened, and about the subsequent heel turn of "THE IMMORTAL" VON "THE ICONS" MENTOR and coach, and of SEXXXY EDDY'S betrayal of their greatest hero.

There was a hushed frenzy within the crowd as EDDY produced a microphone that he had purchased earlier that day and began to speak.

"So, now you know". He began powerfully. "Now you know who the men are, that run these streets. Your Immortal Hero is gone, this time forever" The Sex Symbol said. "He thought, he believed, that I was his friend. You all believed, that I was his friend". Eddy said using his first finger to pan the crowd. "I'm not his friend, and I'm not your friend, in fact, SEXXXY EDDY is so far above your hero that he left your hero laying in a pool of blood, nearly dead.

Soon, very soon in fact, the man who's behind all of this will be here to address you all himself". Eddy said as the opening chorus of Lionel Richies ALL NIGHT LONG played faintly from behind the doors of a local bar. There was a limo sitting idol in the cool black shadows just off of Fullum, its windows tinted and its wet bar fully stocked and loaded. The name on the service slip, was Chris Markem.

Just then, the crowd began to separate like a partisan sea as "THE RICO SUAVE BADBOY" made his way to tonights center stage dressed in a black do rag, diamond studded earring, dark coloured blazer, stubble beard, sun glasses, and form fitting blue jeans. His iconic presence alone was overpowering, earring shimmering in the night. There was a reason why he had been David Danes mentor.

"This for me"?? He asked quickly acknowleding SEXXXY EDDY with a momentary glance before taking the stick from him as Eddy walked away.

There was a sinister riff emanating from somewhere in the distance as if melodiously shadowing the events of the evening. It was around 9:45p.m.

"For those of you who don't know who I am, my name is Chris Markem". The bad man said as chopper propellers whirred in the black sky above. The media was in attendance.

There were signs everywhere-WE WANT VON!!! ONTARIO STREET ORIGINAL AND ETERNAL!!! VON "THE ICON"-MY IMMORTAL ETC.

"Please allow me to introduce myself" Markem said arrogantly. "My name is Chris Markem" He said to a round of palpable hatred. "I'm the one who's responsible for training your hero". He continued smooth as smooth. "I'm also the very reason why David Dane is lying flat on his fuckin back in a hospital bed right now. I put your hero in the hospital like. That's who Von is to all of you"?? Markem questioned as the crowd erupted with cheers that were deafening.

WE, WANT, VON!!! WE, WANT, VON!!! WE, WANT, VON!!! The crowd chanted as flash bulbs went off and spot lights swooned over the spectacle that was taking place on Ontario Streets east end streets.

One sign read ... ... VON "THE ICON"-ONTARIO STREETS VINDICATOR IN THE NIGHT!!!

"This time he's left you for good". THE RICO SUAVE BADBOY boasted to a slew of MARKEM SUCKS!!! Chants followed by a second chorus of –WE WANT VON!!!

"I gave you VON "THE ICON". Markem said, momentarily folding his hands in front of his midsection while still gripping the mic. His brown eyes looked soulless, as if he were morally bankrupt and the results were mirrored in his irises. He almost appeared demonic, crystals smouldering wickedly.

SEXXXY EDDY was outside, center stage, demonstrating a crotch gesture in the direction of the crowd.

"Yeah, you want what every other woman wants"!!! EDDY said licking his lips as he eye balled a thirty something blond. He was doing the gyrating thing now.

"Yeah, I'll come over there and kick you in the face the same way I did VON last night"!!! EDDY threatened looking in her boyfriends general direction.

There was a hushed silence as a stranger appeared from the front seat of a sports coup and began walking.

This had to be Jack. Eddy registered nonchalantly.

BAD was in the air, had been all night.

"I wanna introduce each and every one of you fuckin mutants to my Brother, Jack". THE RICO SUAVE BADBOY said putting an arm around his Brothers shoulders.

Just then Kate "The Gate" Shamrock appeared in the aisle that was created by the separation of the crowd, her beautiful blue eyes were like fused heaters, shimmering, volcanic, as if she were ready to erupt. She had never met Chris Markem before, last night had been a first.

"Oh, look who it is like". Chris Markem said turning his attention to the gorgeous twenty something brunette with the athletic figure.

"Did you come here on behalf of your Uncle or did you come here because you wanted a date"?? Markem asked.

"I think she's lookin for a date". Jack responded. He was smiling, beaming murderously from one ear to the other dressed in a white shirt, black jeans, and cowboy boots. He also had a moustache.

"I wouldn't touch you if you were the last person on earth. You're dead mother fucker"!!! She threatened below an ocean of sound. Heard or not, Kates eyes did the talking for her. She looked vicious.

"Nice to see you". Eddy said closing the distance between them as Kate challenged him to fight.

"I would, but I think the blond over there has other plans for me for the next half hour". THE SEX EXPRESS BOASTED doing the gyrating routine one more time.

"Tell me something Kate, I believe it is?? Why aren't you at the hospital wheeling your Uncle around from one floor to another"??

"Ah … … … … He's in the hospital like". Smiling Jack piped up again.

"Which is where you're gonna be". Kate said approaching Chris Markem, ready to go.

"She can't be serious is she Jackie"?? Chris enquired. "Don't fuck about with me like". The Snake warned taking his blazer off and unbuttoning his shirt and wrist cuffs.

"Ah, C mon Chris. You don't wanna hurt the little bitch do you"??

"So, when do we get to see your fuckin nuisance of an Uncle again like"?? Chris Markem asked looking directly into Kate eyes. She was feverish, poised to kill. This was it, the worst set up and betrayal that she had ever seen, and before all of this, she had heard that Chris Markem was a hero.

"You're like a super hero that's gone bad". Shamrock commented angrily.

"Yeah, well. That's me". Markem retorted, as if trying to make her appear stupid for having said such a thing. He thought she was a fuckin idiot anyway.

"What's the matter, you afraid of a little girl"?? Kate challenged.

Markem nodded condescendingly.

Chris Markem was the most arrogant human being that she'd ever met. What an asshole!!!

"C mon"!!! Shamrock demanded leveling a kick at Markem that he skillfully side stepped.

He had finesse.

"Don't fuckin bug me like". Chris said making a move for his blazer that he had draped over a chair.

"You're a dead man Markem". Kate threatened.

"Hey, that's my little girl". Andrew Dane said coming out of absolutely nowhere to confront his Brothers mentor. He had seen a good portion of their exchange. He was vexed.

"Ah, Jesus Christ, look who it is". Markem acknowledged immediately recognizing his students younger Brother.

Just then EDDY came out of the crowd side kicking Andrew in the skull and knocking him out. He had narrowly missed Barclay who was standing poised with a baseball bat in his hand. "Suck me"!!! THE EXPRESS said putting the boots to Andrews skull.

"FUCK YOU"!!! Kate launched, assaulting EDDY with a spinning heel kick to the chest that sent him careening backward.

Hitting women was not Eddy Dorozowsky's shtick, but here it was. He fucked them, not hit them, and now, finally, someone, a woman mind you, was angry enough to put her hands on him in a way that wasn't sexual.

"Gotta go". He decided disappearing into the growing crowd that was watching sin unfold.

"Yeah, well when David Dane, VON "THE ICON" or whatever he calls himself gets here, we'll have a go like". THE RICO SUAVE BADBOY promised. He had taught David how to fight, and he would dismantle him down to his last vertebrae to.

"C MON"!!! Kate challenged. She was standing above her Father who was lying in a heap. There was an ambulance making its way through the crowd at a crawl now, lights flashing.

"Oh God, Dad, c mon, wake up". She urged as the emergency EMT's made their way toward her fallen Parent. He was bleeding from the mouth and the left nostril.

WE WANT VON!!! WE WANT VON!!! WE WANT VON!!! The chant exploded, but still, there was no sign of their saviour.

"Get him up here". EMT #1 said as he took her Fathers feet and loaded him aboard the stretcher.

"Watch his hands". EMT #2 who had held Andrew Danes head said as he placed the Barristers hands beneath the blanket.

Chris and Jack Markem were laughing maniacally.

"I think we need to wrap this up Jackie". Markem said raising the microphone to his lips.

"I'll see ye soon". He said.

Jonathan Dane had heard about Chris Markems betrayal of his son, and he was ecstatic, nothing could have been anymore melodious to his insidious ears then the news that he had just received. He was sitting in the basement of Cyril Mathews church.

Now, on this unholy evening, he had the satisfaction of knowing that the man that his son had always had undying respect and devotion toward had turned on him.

As always, Jonathan wore his Families trademark smirk that had served to anger so many in the past. He was too many, repulsively sneaky and insidious, with a treacherous penchant for trying to ruin the lives of those that he should have loved most.

Now, on this night, he saw the fever that his son was stricken with, as the best news that he'd gotten in seven decades reached his ears. He had lived, existed, and killed far beyond his era.

Soon, and one way or another, "THE PATH" would seduce his niece and bring her fully into the fold. There was no place for her on the outside, no place for her away from the branch of her Family that should have owned her body, mind, and soul, like an unquenchable fire.

To some, evil was a path they chose to shun, but to Jonathan Dane, it was the way that he lived both inside and out of NIGHT WORLD PRODUCTIONS.

"You've never seen the insides of what we're going to show you here". Cyril Mathews said to the twenty something girl who stood before him with shadows rapidly washing over her face.

He had met her working at an all night atrium on a hill top with bright silver lighting and smoked mirrors, she had taken to him immediately, begging to be fucked by The Devils tongue, well tonight, she would get her wish, and he would show her a duplicate of her soul from the other side.

"Do you want to be my child"?? He asked disrobing before her and showing her his penis.

She was nodding now, caressing him, as his eyes smiled wickedly in the reflection of her irises.

"Will you kill for me after tonight"?? He asked.

Again, she was nodding, sick little vicious things in her pretty eyes. Breath of shadows, winds of fire, Satan be mine!!!

Jonathan Dane was sipping blood from a brass goblet.

Soon, a second man came to take the woman from behind and they began to move rhythmically together back and forward in a single motion.

There were moans now, and gasps as she began to orgasm. She would in no time drink from their cup, unencumbered by the realms of civilisation that had made most unlike her.

"Fuck me"!!! She hollered with a penis caressing her cheek as another penetrated her.

"I want to take you somewhere after we're done here". Cyril suggested. "I want to take you to a house where a Family lives". He suggested in a horrible voice.

"I'll go wherever you want Father". She agreed. "Take me" … … … … … … … …

In half an hour, Cyrils driver parked the van owned by NIGHT WORLD PRODUCTIONS across the street from a two story cedar house with twin chimneys and softly glowing windows. All who occupied it were asleep in their beds, there were two small children and a Mother and Father inside.

"These are the keys to the back door. There are two locks, a night bolt and a tumbler. I want you to go inside, first to the Parents room, upstairs. I want you to cut their throats, after that, I want you to go to the childrens rooms, and I want you to do the same to them. Do you understand Marissa"??

"Hmm hmm". She responded hypnotically, as if below the shadow of hypnosis.

"Good, there's a knife in this rag". Cyril instructed, presenting her with the tool that she would need to dispatch the Family that they had come to see.

"The childrens names are Blaise and Anthony. Their Parents betrayed me". Cyril finished as Marissa de boarded the van and began her journey across the darkened street and around the back of the house where one pilot light glowed smoothly over the panelling of a doorway … … … … … … … …

In his sleep, David Dane saw the house where his Fathers Parents had lived for decades. It was an old white house with chipped paint and a lower door leading onto a basement where Danes Grand Father had kept his workshop for more than thirty years often using it to construct homemade gifts for his grandchildren, or fashion a tool to assist him in his day to day life.

Tonight, in this nightmare, the house was lonely and dark, and wreaked of grease from an unknown origin. There were no occupants remaining, only the sound of ghosts of dreams and moments long ago lived by people who no longer existed.

"Hello". Dane called, but no one entered the answered him inside of this dream brought on by his concussed state.

Then, someway, somehow, his Grand Mother was there again, there in that house, as she had been in her final stages of Alzheimers with her nurse pouring over her, only now she could speak and was warning him of wicked, evil atrocities that were to come.

This was Chezzetcook, but not The Chezzetcook that David Dane had known.

Then, from a closet space, his Grand Father appeared out of nowhere wielding his cane as if fearing an attack from an invisible assailant. He also, had been dead for years, however the room still smelled of pipe smoke and tobacco from Geralds daily habit.

"It's you. So tis". He greeted in his own way. He had been a Farmer and a Mill worker, and Danes favourite Aunt, MARY, The angel of all that was right and special in this world had been his sister. She may have been the greatest person who had ever lived, at least it was indeed possible.

"Hello". He said, as Gerald began to lead the way up the stairs toward a kitchen that was filled with grey smoke and swirls of ancient history.

"Is there fire"?? David Dane had asked listening to invisible wind chimes somewhere in the distance.

Gerald was nodding now. He had stopped smiling. Something was wrong, very wrong.

"So tis". Gerald said again.

"I don't know how I got here". David Dane admitted.

"It's alright. I don't know how you got here either". Gerald said with a chuckle.

Somewhere there was fire, a smouldering, evil, wicked inferno and they were nearing it.

"I still remember this house". Dane said allowing his late Grand Father to lead the way. Rose Buds, his Grand Father had always bought him rose buds as a child and had them waiting when he arrived.

"Do you remember that space up there"?? His Grand Father asked pointing to an attic that existed above the entry way to the basement.

"I do". David Dane responded.

"They bury the dead up there now". Gerald said. "All those strange people that you and I know".

Just then someone on the other side adjusted the pillow that was behind David Danes head.

"You're not doing yourself any favors sticking around here. You're still a young fella". Gerald said of the 40yr. old Dane. "What about you?? Are you going to stick around here"?? Dane asked.

Gerald chuckled. "Ola, and I don't have any choice". He said, back slightly bent with Arthritis that had plagued him for decades prior to his death that was brought on by pneumonia.

"Wake him up. He's slipping into a coma". A nurse who was at David Danes bedside said.

The fire was raging out of control now, flames everywhere, and Gerald was lying on the floor being eaten by the live heat. "It's time for you to go". He whispered from his position on the ground. "This place is no good for you".

"I can't find my way out alone. Come with me". Dane requested.

"C mon Uncle Von. Wake up"!! Kate pleaded emotionally, as her Uncles eye lids twitched and flickered, still dreaming of the flames. It was for him another time and another place. Things that had perished so many years ago now coming to light again. He had watched so many loved ones live and die. This was a memory of their passing, and in a way, a tribute to them.

"Get out of the way". One of the nurses ordered as they pulled the curtain all the way around her legendary Uncles bed.

It was fusing together now, somewhere. And then he was at The Wag Waltic Sail Boat Club as a child, where he had taken swimming and Tennis lessons early on, still cold there, freezing, and the tiny ripples across the surface of the swimming pool below the main house wreaked of Chlorine.

"I don't want to get in there this morning". He had told his Mother as he stood there with his red towel enveloping his shoulders. There was a tractor of some kind humming across the lawns in the distance keeping The WAGS grassy Knowles neat and green.

"C mon Uncle Von, wake up"!!! Kate cried. She was going to kill Chris Markem and SEXXXY EDDY when she saw them. "Please wake up". She pled.

Markem, Eddy, and Jack strolled across the top floor of a mall that's every angle seemed to boast piercing silver dream lights that were nearly blinding. This was a conspiracy that had seen its roots born months and months in advance and put into action within a few hours.

"You think David was surprised like"?? Chris asked beaming proudly from ear to ear.

There was a sign that read SWENSONS behind them.

"I think that Von got the surprise of a life time". The SEX EXPRESS replied wearing a camouflaged top over denim jeans that were tucked into his boots. He also sported a neatly trimmed beard that was freshly grown.

Chris Markem glanced at a gorgeous blond who was walking by. "I should try my usual pick up line on her like. I'll bet David couldn't eat her up. He'd need me to reel her in".

"Ye think he'll be disappointed"?? Jack asked smiling one of his trademark-"I'm smiling, but what's on my mind is murdering you". Grins.

Both Chris and Jack had always been popular with the opposite sex.

"I remember this one time when I was in a Hotel room with a bunch of guys and a girl and everybody in the room wanted her. They left, I stayed. She got to know me better than any of them that night". THE RICO SUAVE BADBOY boasted.

"I'm gonna get David to have a go at me". Chris assured. "He was always a good little scrapper like, but I'll do em in. He's only so good. I taught him, but I didn't teach him everything". He said using another of his trademark catch phrases.

"Ah ... ... we'll see what he does". Jack commented. "What Chris leaves behind, we'll let Eddy here have". Jack said rubbing to top of Eddys dome with the palm of his hand.

At the same time, across town, two solidly built, completely identical African/ Canadian/ American Body Builders were exiting a shiny black Cadillac Sports Coup and heading for the emergency doors of Montreal General Hospital underneath the hood of a low morning sky.

"Hey, watch that, that's my ride and joy". Robert Gray politely reminded a six foot something Hockey thug who was exiting his own car that was adjacent to his.

"I still can't believe that Chris would do that". Robert remarked power fisting the push button to the side of the glass doors that read EMERGENCY in bold red print with adequate force.

"He's supposed to know better. That's his student". Richard responded.

There were two Security guards exiting the building now, each carrying a cup of piping hot Coffee in their hands.

"He put Dane in the hospital. We can't let him get away with that". Robert explained upon entrance to the triage and intake region of the hospitals first floor.

"Elevator's there". Robert said pointing.

144

When they came to the ninth floor dressed in three quarter length black leather jackets over dress slacks they found their friend of twenty five years laid up with tubes running out of him.

"Dane". Robert said leaning in to readjust his friends pillow.

Richard was frowning now. The smiling had stopped.

"Look what they did". The big man said in a low voice.

"I know". Robert answered. "He went too far".

"Can you hear us"?? Richard asked, speaking directly into their friends ear.

Von was nodding now, sedate, somewhere between here and there. He had heard Roberts voice, but couldn't quite understand what was being said to him. "Urdges" He managed, half awake, half dreaming.

"I can't understand why Chris and Jack would wanna do this. Chris is supposed to be your coach". Robert said surveying the litany of tubes that were running in and out of his friend, of their friend. Then somewhere there was the sound of water like a sink running, and he was taken back to the day that the three of them had met, and how Chris had been a part of that too.

They had met Dane while he was sitting on a weight bench at the local Y.

"Hey man, I hear that you have a problem with my Brother and I". Robert had introduced. "I think that we better go upstairs to the locker room and have a talk about this". He said to a surprised looking Dane who had absolutely no idea what he might have said or done to offend either one of these mammoth individuals.

When they got upstairs, behind the door to the changing room, Richard and Robert had acted like they were about to knuckle up when there was the sound of a commode flushing in one of the stalls.

"I wonder who that could be". Robert said letting a Devilish laugh escape him.

"We're your coachs friends". Robert said giving up the rib as Chris Markem came strolling out of one of the bathroom stalls with a smile on his face. "Relax like David, this is Richard and Robert". Markem said humoured that Dane had fallen for their prank hook, line, and sinker.

It was a memorable introduction, and one that "The Immortal" VON "THE ICON" would never forget.

Now, they sat here next to Danes hospital bed with tubes running in lines out of their friend as machines went beep, beep, beep, all around them, courtesy of THE RICO SUAVE BADBOY himself.

Just then Kate returned to her Uncles room, tired, exhausted, and toting a cup of black coffee. There were grey circles around her pretty eyes.

"You have to be Richard and Robert". Shamrock surmised.

"If you say so". Richard said casually sitting back on his chair.

"You guys must have been watching the news back east".

Robert nodded. "Any idea why Mr. Markem would wanna do this"?? Robert asked sarcastically. He was all but disgusted with Chris.

"I don't know. Chris Markem, The Rico Suave BADBOY"!!! Kate said sarcastic as sarcastic.

"Why would Chris do this"?? Robert asked.

"Because the man's an asshole". Kate responded. "He's supposed to be this big legend, and then he goes and does this. My Father's sitting at home with a concussion because SEXXXY EDDY knocked him out with a kick".

"Yeah, I think someone needs to speak to Chris. That, and I'm in a bad mood now".

"Yeah, no shit". Kate said sniffling lightly before pulling up a chair next to the bed.

"So what happens now"?? Gate asked.

"We go and see your Uncles coach". Richard replied sternly.

Chris Markem sat at the foot of the stage of an upscale strip club that's owner was a friend of his from back east who also moonlighted as a broker. Markem was in a somber mood. He had done what he had set out to do here in Montreal. This was a HOSTILE TAKEOVER the magnitude of which David Dane had never seen in his life. Before it was all over, there would be bloodshed in the streets, particularly those in the east end.

"Slip me another Boiler Maker". THE RICO SUAVE BADBOY ordered the female cocktail waitress who Markem believed had "Substantial Endowments", a favorite terminology of his from years gone by. He had always liked women, particularly the ones who catered to his every need and fantasy.

"Ah, Chris". Jack greeted lightly from behind his Brother".

"Look at the fuckin rack on that dancer". Chris said, lazily pointing in her direction. "I should ask her to leave with me". He said as reflections from the clubs strobe lights danced across the walls.

"I just got a phone call". Jack told him".

"Yeah, from who like"??

"Richard and Robert". He said turning to look over his shoulder at the empty club around them that was bathed in a pale blue wash like an indoor sky.

"Oh, yeah. What did they want like"??

"They wanna meet us later on today, so I told them that we'd be here for a while like". The younger of the two Markems said firming himself up on his seat.

On Jacks last word, Richard and Robert came strolling through the main doors of the club casually approaching their long time comrades from behind.

"What's up Chris"?? Robert said lightly slapping Markem on the back of the shoulders.

"Hey, good to see you". Chris greeted twisting his glance over his right shoulder as Richard and Robert took a seat on opposite sides of him.

"What brings you guys to Montreal"?? The Boxing Legend asked.

"You do". Robert answered. "Your student's in the hospital ... ... You know anything about that"?? One half of THE BROTHERS FROM THE GHETTO asked, chomping on a piece of gum.

Chris leaned back, adjusting the position of his foot against the edge of the stage. There was tension in his body language, and Smiling Jack had stopped smiling.

"I put him there". Markem admitted.

"Yeah, that's what we heard". Robert said quickly shooting a glance toward the half naked dancer who was leaving the stage.

"Why'd you put em there"?? Richard, who had always been close to Chris questioned.

"He's a fuckin mu ... ...

"Shouldn't ah done that". Robert scolded, no longer affable in tone. "Next time we hear about you going near David Dane, I don't know Chris. We're gonna have to do something about it".

"Yeah, you do that like". Markem warned, placing a tooth pick between his lips.

"Ah C mon, you guys don't really care about him that much do you"?? Jack questioned. The sinister smile had returned.

"You threaten me again, you're a dead man". Chris explained.

"My Brother's a what"?? Richard demanded. "You wanna step outside Chris"?? Rich asked.

Markem was up righting himself in his chair now.

"Go, leave it alone". The Boxing Icon and Champion said.

Robert and Richard had lost their sense of humour, it was just going to take a little more, the smallest of nudges and the four of them would be outside, throwing down. Chris and Jack had gotten away with enough already.

"Okay Chris, but if you give us one more reason, it's on"!!! Robert warned as he and Richard raised from their seats minus their customary good mood.

"We'll see". Markem said as Robert and Richard disappeared out the same doors as they had entered.

In David Danes dream he saw himself training on the bag behind Chris Markems Mothers house in Spryfield. This was a dream of silence without sound.

In each image Dane saw himself obeying Chris Markems every command throwing jabs, right hands, left hooks, right crosses, as well as a series of combinations to Markems muted words.

Chris Markem had not only trained David Dane, he had mentored him in style, mannerism, physical prowess, finesse, as well as ability. There was no part of Danes repertoire back then that did not come from the man that he considered to be his idol. Dane was indeed, and with pride, a product of Chris Markem.

The next image saw Dane, Markem, and Markems then girlfriend leaving an apartment complex on Old Sambro Road. Markem was as always dressed to the nines from head to toe from the diamond stud in his left ear to his white dress shirt, and perfectly tailored dress pants. He looked like a movie star, thus the nickname "HOLLYWOOD"!!!

It would have been Christmas Day 1993 when that had happened, and Dane was uncharacteristically tipsy but not drunk.

Chris had at one point placed his diamond stud in Danes ear as a sign of passing the torch.

Now, years later, Markem was a different man with a head full of bad intentions, which is how he had taught Dane to hit.

"Bad is in the blood". Dane saw himself mouthing just as Chris Markem embraced him.

"You'll be a good little scrapper one day like". He recalled Markem saying.

Dane had always been proud of the fact that he'd been chosen as The Legendary Rico Suave BADBOYS successor. Even to this day, he still boasted about it whenever and wherever he got the chance. He loved his coach. There was zero denying it.

Now, he was awake, sitting and staring at the beige wall just past the folded curtain in his hospital room, and Kate was there to, sleeping. She had probably been up all night keeping mad vigilant of him.

"Good morning angel eyes". Von "The Icon" said, jarring his niece back to the conscious realm.

"Oh my God, Uncle Von"!!! Kate "The Gate" Shamrock celebrated elated that her hero had seemingly risen from the dead, for a second time. He was like a cat with nine lives, it only worried her that he'd already used up too many.

"How long have I been out"?? Ontario Streets Immortal Legend asked stretching his arms way above his head and bringing them slowly back into place, ease up, quiet, yet awake.

"A few days. You had a serious concussion".

"Yeah, someone decided to test the durability of my skull" ....

"You had a couple of visitors from back east". Kate explained leaning half way in to embrace her favorite Uncle before hearing a voice at her back.

"Nah, you have a couple of visitors from back east". Robert Gray said entering the room from the hallway. Richard was only steps behind him. "What's up Dane"?? Robert asked letting a huge, familiar smile escape him, and in Danes current state of affairs, it was like a ray of sun.

"Apparently I am". Ontario Streets Prodigal son responded.

"We just spoke to your coach". Robert informed him.

Danes smile evaporated. "Yeah, I remember seeing him, and Eddy" … … … … … … … …

"Who's Eddy"?? Richard asked pulling up a chair beside the railing of Danes bed.

"SEXXXY EDDY". Kate said straightening her Uncles pillow. "Or at least he thinks he's sexy". She said.

"What would make Chris Markem do a thing like this"?? Von asked seriously. He could not fathom how he and Chris Markem could have ended up on opposite sides of the fence, they had been Father and Son, Teacher and student, forever … … … … … …

"We don't know". Rich said.

"It looks like Chris has gone HOLLYWOOD, if you know what I mean". Robert surmised.

Just then a nurse came in to survey Dane who was finally awake.

"That's mine". Rich said lifting his bag from a chair that rested by the window.

My God these two men were huge!!! The Nurse noticed. They were like mountains, and of muscle.

Just then Kates cell phone lit up. It said "Grand Dad" … … … … … … … … …

"I came here because I wanted you to see this". Jonathan Dane said standing in the parking lot in the rising sun. He had a dagger in his hand. "I want you to watch". He said biting down on his lower jaw as he brought the blade of the knife across his throat severing his own wind pipe before crumpling to the ground as his black robe flowed out around him like an oil spill.

Kates hands were covering her mouth now as she continued the bare witness to the end of sin.

The shadows from the sun that was soon to act as a heater for the day were all around her now. She had just witnessed her Fathers, Father commit suicide in front of her very eyes as the minions who had once congregated around her Grand Father somewhere moaned in a collective unison as if signalling the end of a nightmare that began with one Fathers sadism.

"Kate"!!! Andrew called from behind her.

"Daddy"!!! She shouted, turning and screaming as she ran into her Fathers arms. "How did you know"?? She asked as Andrew grimly held up his cellphone. She could vaguely make out the wording of the text message that had brought her Father here.

Wake from My Realm. Played in the far off distance of her mind somewhere.

"He's gone". Andrew said holding his Daughter against his left side and shoulder. "He's gone". He said as blood from Jonathan Danes arteries spread out across the earth.

SEXXXY EDDY stood in the basement of The Police Station being printed dressed in a blazer and form fitting jeans as he threatened the cops with his press agent.

"You know who I am?? I'll be outta here by noon you civil servant mother fucker". Pro Wrestlings SEXXXY Bad Boy said delivering an out of ring promo.

"You think you're gonna hold me on a basic assault charge?? Why aren't the womens groups screaming?? Because I already fucked them all. I'm SEXXXY EDDY Officer Jack Off. You can't best me, you can't arrest me"!!! He said.

"You're not standing in a Ring Mr. Dorozowsky. This isn't a wrestling show" Officer Blakewood reminded him although it was a thrill to be in the presence of an athlete that he'd idolized for so long.

"I know where I am you stupid bastard. It's you and your miserable job that are in jeopardy. Just throw me in a cell with Tamara Sytch and I'll be just fine". The Boastful Bachelor bragged.

"At least he's wearing clothes". Officer Williams said. He was familiar with Eddys in ring character.

"You know what this means"?? Eddy said being walked to a holding cell in hand cuffs. "This means no more free passes to the next show. Well, at least I'll have your lowlife, I mean wife, all to myself. Don't worry, I'll show Karen a good time". Eddy said of Officer Mike Williams better half, and to SEXXXY EDDY, she was indeed better.

Williams was shaking his head now. He could not believe the audaciousness of this particular detainee.

When they got a few steps further, Officer Williams cell phone lit up like a fiery orange crystal. "Yeah, we're taking him to his cell now. Who is it"?? Williams asked.

EDDY was still beaming like a beacon. "What is it, my female lawyer?? I knew Carla couldn't stay away".

"Be quiet"!!! Williams ordered indignantly as he led EDDY passed a cross dressed hermaphrodite.

"I HAVE A CONDOM HUNNY"!!!! EDDY shouted into the mouth piece of the phone.

"Looks like you're outta here". Williams exclaimed. "You must have friends in high places".

"Who posted my bail, Justin Trudeau"?? Eddy asked quizzically.

"Someone named Gray". The Officer said.

Damian walked into a shady park in the cities west end with a bad feeling in the pit of his stomach. He had a scheduled rendezvous with a man in about fifteen minutes. There would be no shying away from the topic that they were going to discuss, evil or not.

He had ridden this horse to its gate. There was no going any further. His full end was about to come back and bite him in the ass, by hook or by crook. There were going to be consequences.

You only did these things, played these games, and burnt bridges for so long, before someone, somewhere decided to burn you, and if things didn't go exactly according to plan, these wicked little things were going to burn The Gargoyle From The Gates Of Hell himself to the remnant of ashes.

Up until this point he had been all that any person with a weakness for narcotics had to fear. Now, finally, he was the target. He was, for once, the hunted, and he had no one to blame but himself.

"Damian". A voice echoed from behind him, as the tree tops overhead swished and sloshed in unison in the wind.

"I told you I'd be here Angus". He said to the six foot something Scotsman with the white hair and sun glasses who was, if nothing else, the owner of his very soul at this point. Truth be told, Angus owned Damian, period!!!

"I'm not gonna do it Angus. I'm not gonna kill Von".

"You're not going to what"?? Angus asked, rude and displeased. "You were paid up front to do this job, now you're trying to walk away from us". Angus scolded through his thick accent that's roots were back home in a town called Ayrshire.

"I can't do something like that". Damian said removing his blue tooth from behind his left ear and dropping it to the earth below him. "Besides, I don't have it in me, and I talk to Von on a regular basis, so" … … … … … … … … …

"Where's our money"?? Angus demanded pulling on a pair of stretchy black gloves over his pale fingers.

"I spent it". Damian conceded truthfully. "I even bought a sea-do". He said being a brazen smart ass. "Hey, I hit this one wave" … … … … … …

Now there was a slight drizzle between them, raining down, getting harder, accelerating.

"I'm gonna have to kill you for that lad". Angus embarked. "I'm sorry about that".

The snakes were out in full force.

"I was afraid I might die today". Damian said reaching into his waist band and pulling out a Gloc Nine Semi- Automatic that he pointed directly at the dangerous Scotsman. "Now, you have a choice Angus Beef. You can turn around and go play the fuckin bag pipes, or you can die like a loser here in this park. It's gonna be your choice, but either way, I'm gonna use this gun".

"You're gonna be on the run after tonight Damie". Angus warned as the rain sped up.

"Yeah, well, shit happens". Damian explained tightening his grip on the trigger as Angus began to back away. No matter, he would do it anyway, and steal Angus's pocket book at the same time, watch, wallet and whatever else this weathered Scottish Mobster was holding.

"Bye Angus". Damian said squeezing the trigger and watching Angus crumple onto the green grass just steps from a stone foot bridge that Damian had once stood below.

"Thank, you, very much".

Damian said examining the gun that was supposed to have been used in the murder of Von "The Icon" before chambering it and disappearing over the very foot bridge from which he had originally appeared.

When SEXXXY EDDY reached the front doors of The Police Station there were two Hard core, bad to the bone, African Canadian Body Builders waiting for him on either side of an attractive jet black Cadillac Sports Coup that had been polished to its chrome and silver standing in the rain.

"What's up SEXXXY"!!! Robert Grey toyed with a squinting glare in his eyes.

"Not much. Are you guys fans"?? The SEX EXPRESS asked carefully descending the front steps of the precinct and stepping down onto the sidewalk. He looked slightly more than worse for wear.

"Big fans". Richard said walking around and opening the passenger door for EDDY to climb in.

"You want me to get in"?? EDDY asked suspiciously. These guys looked like bad dudes dressed in T-Shirts, Do Rags, and Body Building pants.

"Who are you guys"??

"We're your benefactors. We're part of a watch dog group for wrestlers who get themselves into trouble with the law". Rich said bobbing up and down with a ridiculously exaggerated excitement in his step.

"Watch Dog Group"?? EDDY asked.

Robert was nodding confidently now. "We're like Angels Of Mercy". He said.

"Good Samaritans". Rich enforced. "C mon, get in. It's getting wet outside".

EDDY shrugged, it was a brave new world. Maybe these guys really did have his best interest at heart.

In a few minutes the three of them were on the road with Rich driving, Robert in the passenger seat, and EDDY in the back seat blissfully listening to his head set.

Robert was eating a Big Mac.

"Hey Rich, they should've put more Ketchup on this Hamburger". Robert complained.

"Hey EDDY, you alright back there"?? Rich asked glancing at their passenger in his rear view mirror as he leaned slightly to turn a corner.

EDDY was nodding. "Thanks for bailing me out. Say, what are your names again"?? EDDY asked as a sheet of rain slid down the windshield and was then attacked by the windshield wipers.

"Guns N Roses". Robert replied. "Well, they call us Guns and Roses but actually on the mic we sound a little more like Elton John". He responded affably.

"No seriously". EDDY asked beginning to wonder if he should've agreed to accept this ride after all. These guys seemed to be a bit evasive when it came to their identities.

"You really wanna know"?? Robert asked having totally dropped his sense of humour. "Robert and Richard Gray". He said as Rich also began to adopt his Brothers more serious demeanour.

Robert and Richard Gray. Eddy had heard both of those names somewhere before.

"Say, you know Von "The Icon"?? Rich asked lethally serious now, and again, he was staring at EDDY in the rear view whose pigmentation had turned to an off shade of, well, … … … … … … … grey.

There was utter silence for a moment as the Cadillac that was Roberts ride and joy came to a halt below a cement canopy near the Old Port rain pitter-pattering on its roof.

"Get out"!!! Richard ordered.

"Huh"?? Eddy asked as Robert exited the passenger seat and knuckled up.

"What do you guys want"?? Dorozowsky asked sliding across the back seat and exiting the stylish automobile legs first, torso second.

"What do we want"?? Robert asked. "I don't know. What do we want Rich"?? He asked glaring violently at Eddy who now looked like he might pass out. He must have been giving away at least a hundred pounds to each one of these thugs.

"I'm gonna show him". Rich explained. "You can start by getting on your fuckin knees". The Former Club Bouncer from Grey Stone said smashing EDDY in the face, and dropping him to the cement.

"Hey, it's your turn man". Rich said in the direction of his twin Brother.

Robert was again nodding, chomping away on a piece of gum.

155

"Look out SEX MAN"!!! Robert said dancing backward in an overly exaggerated boxer posture and leveling EDDY with a hand strike to the face that sent him crashing to the rain slicked pavement minus half a cup of blood.

"He's bleeding from the mouth". Rich commentated. "I think you need to make his head match his lips, that's what I think".

Robert nodded. "I know". He said lifting EDDY to his feet and dropping him with a wicked right to the side of the forehead. "Now, we need to have a little talk about your real benefactor. You see that tree over there"?? Robert asked commanding EDDYS full attention.

EDDY was on all fours now, clutching his chest and nodding as a string of blood hung from his lower lip.

"If we ever hear of you or your benefactor fucking up David Dane again, we're gonna bury you underneath it, you understand"?? Robert said leaning down to get eye level with SEXXXY EDDY who wasn't so sexy anymore.

"Here, go clean up". Rich said tossing EDDY a white rag.

"Goodnight"!!! Both men said simultaneously.

That night under a black sky Chris and Jack Markem stood side by side flanked by Scott Paris and Troy Barclay who were both wielding baseball bats at the threat of an onslaught by whomever as retribution for what they'd done.

As everyone in the neighbourhood was gathered around there was a sound like a surge of energy that was produced by two electronic devices that had been strategically placed at opposite ends of the street late that afternoon.

Suddenly, as the streetlights died all at once there was a sound like a bird or a crow cawing somewhere in the distance followed by an ominous voice over from deep in the night.

"As darkness falls over a once proud empire, a hero rises from settled ash to face his enemies, a vindicator amongst gathered dusk, the hero returns to destroy those who attempted to silence his voice forever. Ladies and gentlemen … … … … … This, is, … … … … … … VON … … … … … … "THE ICON" … … … … … … … The transmission from darkness ended as Ontario Streets Hero ascended into the center of the fray strapped to a cord that was wrapped around his waist. There was a led pipe in his hand reflectively shimmering and shining in the twilight.

"He's here"!!! Markem yelled as "THE IMMORTAL" VON "THE ICON" attacked all four of his enemies with the pipe that Lilly had once given him as a gift for use as a weapon.

Paris and Barclay were back pedaling now as VON and CHRIS locked eyes in the center of the night.

VON v.s. MARKEM!!!, one sign read in bold black print.

Richard and Robert were exiting their sports car now, doors slamming shut behind them.

Chris, and Jack, Scott Paris, and Troy Barclay were making a mad dash for their car that they had parked at the curb. As soon as they were inside Barclay twisted the key in the ignition and floored the red Camaro into a U-Turn, in an attempt to flee the scene.

"Yeah, you better leave Chris". Robert said watching the Camaro turn away and vanish into the night.

Von was staring in the direction of Richard and Robert now. His face was straight as he nodded "THANKS" to his friends of twenty five years who had stopped in to help him at just the right time.

"No problem Dane". Robert responded doing his trademark bounce on both feet, fists clenched.

The battle between good and evil, had begun!!!

CHAPTER VI

"**D**avid's gonna pay for that like". THE RICO SUAVE BADBOY threatened, as he, Scott Paris, Troy Barclay, Jack, and a wounded SEXXXY EDDY entered a seedy looking night club through the back door.

"I have your money". Chris informed the six foot five doorman who was covered in tattoos.

"Thanks". Milo said accepting a hand full of fresh bills. He had no sense of humour, and humanity was a far cry from his depth. He was a stone killer. He had been known to hurt people, really hurt people, even smash them into a thousand pieces, but tonight, he was simply a D man.

"Good to see you like". Smiling Jack said removing his wind breaker and folding it across the back of a chair. "EDDY here needs a drink. What's your fix"?? Jack enquired.

"Scotch". He responded still in visible pain.

"So Robert and Richard gave you something to fret over like"?? Jack asked him. "Ah, don't worry. We'll take care a that. Me and Chris are better than average scrappers". He said, and indeed they were far above average.

"So, you're Brother won titles"?? EDDY enquired.

"We went all around Alberta in a car. Chris was trained by a man named Rex Clues". Jack explained, matter of fact. "My Brother trained David. If it wasn't for Chris, there would be no HERO for ONTARIO STREETS people to cheer for. I was there. I remember walking around the garage below The Danes house with my Brothers. I can still remember the bag hanging from the ceiling over there. Chris knocked it down".

"Knocked what down"?? THE RICO SUAVE BADBOY asked sitting down.

"The bag in David Danes basement". Jack responded through his customary murderous smile. He was, without effort, completely intimidating.

"Fuckin mutant!!! I'm gonna give David three good reasons to get plastic surgery". Markem threatened, unimpressed.

"Just three"?? Jack quipped.

"His face, his head, and at least one of his eyes like, then me and Jackie here are gonna deal with Richard and Robert. They won't be twins after we're done with them, at least not that anyone'll be able to tell".

Jack was chuckling now. "We're finally gonna find out who'd win that fight like". Smiling Jack said.

When VON "THE ICON" entered his town house later that night he found Marilyn Dane resting on the couch with the T.V. set on. There was a forest fire raging on the screen before her.

"What's wrong with Nana"?? KATE "THE GATE" SHAMROCK asked standing in the center of her Uncles living room with WARRIOR at her knee. He had just come in from one of his WARRIOR walks, eaten dinner, and was now completely exhausted.

"I have no idea. I think she should be taken to a Doctor". THE IMMORTAL ONE said.

Marilyn Dane had not spoken a word since they'd brought her home.

"Did you call Ray"?? VON asked.

"Yeah, and Damian called. He wants to talk to you".

"Damian"?? VON asked, surprised.

"Whatever he wanted it sounded urgent, not like he was home relaxing with a beer in his hand".

"Fuck"!!! VON lamented dialing Damians cell number.

"Yeah". Damian answered in a shaky voice, cabaret singer smooth. VON had always thought that Damian sounded like a vocalist, almost like John Secada, or that guy who used to be on General Hospital with the long hair. VON could not recall the Spanish talents name, but he had gone on to become very famous.

What the hell was it??

"I shot somebody". Damian immediately confessed.

"Is this a clean line"?? VON asked wondering what the fuck would ever possess Damian to admit to such a crime over a phone even if the line was clean.

"Where are you"??

"I'm at what the fuck do you call it, Terminus Voyager". Damian said of the bus terminal that stood at one end of Berri Park and ran off of ST. HUBERT and DE MAISSONEUVE.

"Can you come and meet me"?? Damian asked.

"Meet me in the underground in thirty". VON agreed.

ROBERT AND RICHARD- At this time I wanna break in to acknowledge two of the best people that I've ever known on this planet, Robert and Richard Gray.

I also know that both of you guys have kids so I want to speak directly to them now. Both of your Fathers are heroes, and not fake heroes, but people who live up to their images every day of their lives both in and out of the presence of others. I've never met two finer examples of what a human being should be on this earth, and I'll tell ye, with my at times critical attitude toward people, that's not something that you'll hear me say every day.

Richard and Robert-You guys have inspired me not only in the gym but in my basic life as well. You've never betrayed our friendship, nor let me down in any discernible way. I've been referred to as an icon, but both of you guys are far more deserving of that title then I am. You were my role models growing up and now your kids are gonna benefit from having you both as Fathers. I love and respect you both, and to me, our relationship goes a lot further than friendship. I think of you both as Family.

I'm gonna shut up now before you guys decide to whoop me when you see me for being too sentimental.

Thank you for all that you ever did for me, and for always treating others with the same respect.

Regards,
VON "THE ICON",
FROM-"THE ONTARIO STREET ORIGINAL" TO YOU
4 LIFE!!!

"You shot somebody"?? VON "THE ICON" asked incredulously. He couldn't believe the story that his ears, and Damians mouth were telling him. This was astounding. Von had never seen Damian get violent with anyone, much less shoot them.

"I shot him in the face and in the eye". He said. "Well, I guess that technically the face is the eye, one way or another, you know what I mean". The French Italian Indian said. He was a bit tired looking.

"Jesus". Von remarked rubbing his forehead with the palm of his hand. "Well did anyone see you do it"?? The Immortal Legend asked raising his eye brows unconsciously.

"I don't think so, probably not".

"Probably not, because if any one saw you, then we're going to have a problem on our hands".

"Well, I would say that most likely nobody saw me". Damian concluded standing in the deepening shadows between two Grey Hound buses. They were just outside the terminal in the underground parking lot that spilled out onto a main through fare.

"I think that nobody saw me".

"Let's hope The Prosecutor feels the same way".

"Listen, if I go to jail will you deposit some canteen money … … … … … …??

Von was going to shoot Damian himself.

"This is ridiculous". The Icon said.

"It's not that ridiculous".

There was a bus exiting the car port a few feet away from them.

"Have you ever met my Brother"?? Von asked wondering at what point his friend was going to require the services of a lawyer, and one that he couldn't pay for at that.

"They wanted you to kill me"?? The Boxer asked.

"Yes".

"And you told them yes"?? Von asked disbelievingly, as if either Damian was crazy for telling him this or he was crazy for listening.

"I had to find a way to get them to give me the money".

"So, you lied to them"??

"Von, do you think they would've given me any money if I'd told them the truth?? That would've completely defeated the purpose".

"Which was what, to get us both killed"??

"That's being too melodramatic".

"No one should ever have taught you how to speak English". Von remarked walking in the other direction with his hands on his hips.

"Why not"??

"Because it makes you to dangerous".

"There's not a lot of ways to make money in this world". Damian rationally explained, matter of fact.

"So you make false promises to mobsters about carrying out contracts"??

"I guess that maybe I did that".

"Are you guys waiting for a bus"?? A security officer asked coming around the corner between two busses.

"No, we were just on our way out of here".

"Hey, I was gonna do my … … … … … … …

"One more word out of you and they're gonna have to … … … … … … … …

"Alright, let's go". Damian conceded.

"They couldn't have set us up any better like". Chris Markem said with a tooth pick dangling between his lips as he, JACK, SEXXXY EDDY, and two beautiful strippers surveyed the Pent House Suite that over looked the entire downtown core of Montreal.

"WHOAAA"!!! EDDY exclaimed removing a wrapped condom from his jeans pocket. "Who wants to go first ladies"?? THE SEX EXPRESS asked licking his lips.

"I wanna ride The Sex Express". Rochelle admitted. "Which way do you like it"?? She asked lifting her skirt above her hips.

"Take her in the bathroom. Jackie and I have to have a meeting like". Markem said seriously as a SADE song along with the accompanying video played on the television set.

"What about me"?? The second of the two dancers whose name was Samantha asked.

"Who fuckin asked you to speak like"?? THE RICO SUAVE BADBOY asked.

"Fuck you, I'll take my shit and do it someplace else". She said removing a small white packet of powder from her bra. She had copped it from a dealer named YOYO on the way over here.

"Don't say Fuck You to me bitch". The Boxing Legend retorted in a low, ominous voice, bad to the bone.

"You want me to leave"?? She asked dumping a small portion of her shit onto her extended pinky nail before snorting it up one of her nostrils.

"Go"!!! Chris ordered her.

"I'll take them both". EDDY offered, never at a loss for words. He was a ladies man and a nympho maniac to the bone. He had once fucked five strippers in the kitchen of a local steak house after a house show.

Just as EDDY was leading both dancers into the washroom there was a knock on the door.

"Who is it"?? Markem asked lightly scratching the tip of his ear lobe with his first finger.

"It's Paris. Open up"!!! Scott said as Jack crossed the room and opened the door.

"I would've brought beer if I'd known there was gonna be a party". He said.

"Get yourself a seat. Pull up a chair. I'm gonna explain to you how we're going to put an end to David Dane not to mention Richard and Robert" … … … … … … … … … … … … … …

"I don't know who you are, and it's not gonna take an expert for you to put two and two together and make four. I'm gonna kick your ass. That's what I do for a living and then I teach it nine to five. They sent you here because they knew you were good. I don't know what brand of killer you are, but you're about to find out why I sell out arena's across this nation and around the world". Kate said to the leather clad Samoan nightmare who stood before her in the underground parking lot that was awash with piercing silver spot lamps. This woman looked sick, not right in the head, it was in her eyes.

No guard. Where was the fucking guard?? Christ this woman who was circling her was awesome. She was well over six feet, Kate registered leveling a spinning wheel kick in her oppositions general direction.

"Fuck"!!! Kate cursed having connected with no affect.

"Why don't you use this"?? Cyril Mathews asked stepping out of the bright hot silver glare with a nine millimeter Beretta in his hand. He was cloaked in red and black with silver flesh tone covering his face.

"Who the fuck are you and what the fuck do you want"?? Shamrock asked supporting her stance.

"I'm the man that used to work with your Grand Father".

"Fuck my Grand Father. He's dead"!!! She said.

"I want you to kill Kokina"!!! Cyril said extending the hand that held the pistol.

"I don't want the fucking gun. I want her dead and you out of here". Shamrock said stepping back in the direction of two parked automobiles that's owners had likely spent a pretty penny on them. They were glinting, and shine.

"Try this on"!!! Kate said striking Kokina with a wicked front kick that hardly phased her at all.

"Your husband's here to". Cyril said with an intensity in his black eyes that Kate had seen in few other places. He looked like The Devil, only far more malevolent.

"What"?? Kate asked anxiously as she glanced over her right shoulder just on time to see Evan Phillips appear between a Mercedes and a Jag with glare bouncing off of their trunk hoods. He looked sick, sinister, with evil intentions in his tormented eyes.

"You're back from the dead"??

Evan was sneering morbidly now. "Can't be back from where you never were". He said pulling on stretch leather over his hands. Murderous morbidity in human form. There was "Fuck you" on his face. This was enjoyable enough for him. There would never have been a happier time had he returned to his child hood.

"What the fuck do you want"?? Kate asked in a breathy voice.

"In short form?? Your soul"!!! Cyril Mathews explained amidst smouldering eyes. These were The Devils men and this underground parking lot had just become his playground.

In her minds eye Kate saw the twisted, disturbed individual who had been her Grand Father bringing the blade of a knife across his throat in the early morning hours outside of The Montreal General.

"You'll come with us now"!!! Cyril said striking Shamrock across the skull with a heavy blow.

"There's enough pain in my heart to last forever". VON "THE ICON" said sitting on a bench in the big park with the frothing fountains at the foot of The Jaques Cartier Bridge. It was midnight or close to it. He had been out with WARRIOR and Andrew since nine. It was cold outside.

"I'm sorry about the world that Kate was forced to grow up in. She deserved far better than the deal that she got". VON said leaning in slightly to brush something from WARRIORS fur coat.

"I won't disagree with that". Andrew said straightening his blazer that he hadn't removed since he'd returned from work.

The sky overhead was white with thick clouds.

"I'll never get over Lilly's death". VON remarked genuinely. "There are images that no matter what will haunt me forever. It's like the person dies and somehow becomes a part of you. I still remember Lilly coming home at night and changing into her pink T-SHIRT and my grey sweat pants and sitting cross legged in front of the glow of the T.V. I used to put my arms around her and tell her how much I loved her. I'll never forget her fuzzy voice saying "I love you too baby" after she did her hit. That era was the best of my entire life. I used to wait like a kid for her to come home to me, and I'd get so anxious you know" ... ... "She'd always call me from the store downstairs to come and open the door because you needed a key. It's like that key was the key to Heaven, at least for me".

"ROOF"!!! WARRIOR barked in agreement as if he were part of the whole conversation that was going on.

"I should call Leilani". Andrew said standing up and straightening his dress slacks. "You and WARRIOR should get going. It's getting cold outside". He said, switching gears.

"Yeah, we're gonna do another lap around the park and then I think we'll call it a night". THE IMMORTAL ONE said.

At the same time a Street Hooker walked up and smiled a warm smile in the direction of ONTARIO STREETS HERO.

"Hey, how you doin"?? VON asked, glancing in his old friend direction. "You should get inside. You're gonna freeze to death out here". He said.

"Yeah, I know, need my shit otherwise I wouldn't be out here at all. Who's your friend"?? Ann Marilyn asked petting WARRIOR on the head.

"This is the next Prime Minister. At least he's better looking than Steven Harper, don't you think"?? VON asked. "They wanna put a K-9 on Parliament Hill, equal rights and everything" ... ... He said.

166

Just then Andrew Dane came running back to the bench where his Brother and WARRIOR had parked themselves. He looked nervous.

"What's the matter"?? VON asked through puffs of cold, white air.

"One of Jonathans men has Kate. They want you and I in return". Andrew exclaimed.

"Where is she"?? VON asked glancing one way and then another.

"She's in a house about six or seven blocks from here". Andrew said, his voice quivering. "We have to go now" … … … … … … … … …

When both men arrived at the back door of the address that they'd been given they let themselves in using a key that had been placed beneath a door mat that sat below a patio door. This end of the neighbourhood was seedy with lots of Crack Dens, Pimp hold ups, and shooting galleries most of whose entrances were run off of shady alleyways or up long flights of winding stairs that seemingly led to nowhere.

On the ground level there were chain link fences and white picket fences with chipped paint exposing rotted grey wood where stray cats or diseased rats often sat to take refuge from the cold, callous cement and high patches of un-kept grass below. In short, this place almost resembled a junior version of the back streets of Vancouvers Down Town East Side.

"We should have brought WARRIOR with us". Andrew said in a low voice.

"I didn't want him in the middle of all this". David Dane explained.

As they stepped through the back door with its four sections of transparent glass VONs eyes darted around to see what he could see in this silent maze of darkness with whisps of silver light that were provided by bits of piercing glare from the overhead street lamps outside in this day that had turned to night.

"There's a basement door across the room". Von said noticing an off white wooden door.

"Where is she"?? Andrew thought aloud.

VON was pointing in the direction of another room now as a shadow that appeared to be human moved in one direction, and then another.

"Who's there"?? VON asked, but no response followed.

Dreams … … … … … …

"Where's my little girl"?? Andrew yelled as Evan Phillips appeared before him holding a knife to Kates throat. "She's right here Councilor"!!! The Druid Demon said.

"Evan"?? Andrew voiced in disbelief.

"Back from the grave. I'll bet you didn't expect to see me standing in the twilight tonight did you"?? Evan asked.

Andrew was shaking his head now. VONS eyes were smouldering.

"I killed you". ONTARIO STREETS IMMORTAL HERO said.

"Uncle Von". Kate yelled reaching behind Evans neck and flipping him over onto his back.

As Evan rolled himself ass first onto his feet Andrew floored him with a hard blow to the jaw dropping him for all he was worth.

"The parties already started". Cyril Mathews remarked stepping into view beyond the threshold of a nearby door. There was a hand held video camera in his hand. "And you, what the fuck are you doing here again"?? He asked staring at VON who had shaken a concealed knife into his hand.

"NOOO"!!! Andrew hollered charging at Evan before the two crashed through the white door and fell together down a long flight of stairs into a dingy cellar.

"Mathews"!!! VON taunted readying the knife for its use as a murder weapon.

"Kill him Uncle Von"!!! Kate shouted as Mathews casually moved toward him.

VON stepped back distancing himself slightly from the child killer who was moving toward him at a rapid pace. This would hopefully be adequate enough distance. VON thought as he began to shank Mathews in the face and in the chest over and over again drawing massive amounts of blood from the evil little mans silver flesh tone.

Now, there were flames from downstairs as Cyril attempted to rest the knife away from VON "THE ICON" who was now slicing lines across Mathews chest and face, ripping, tearing, and cutting flesh, opening him everywhere.

As the flames rose from the cellar Cyril Mathews fell in a heap on the ground, finally dead.

"DADDY"!!! Kate hollered as her Father emerged from the basement in flames with Evan holding onto his ankle. Both men were in a struggle for their lives now.

"Fuck you mother fucker"!!! Kate shouted violently stepping on her former fiances wrist nearly breaking it in half.

"Let's go"!!! VON yelled as Andrew rolled onto the floor in order to extinguish the flames that had engulfed him. He was screaming now as his older brother jumped on top of him in an effort to smother the fire completely.

"LET'S GO"!!! VON shouted as the entire house began to go up.

As the three reached the back alley Kate was in tears and Andrew was burned in sections down to his flesh. "I love you". He said cradling his Daughter. "I love you"!!!!

"Lifeless hearts don't beat at all". Chris Markem said presiding over Scott Paris and Troy Barclay. It was getting colder, and if THE RICO SUAVE BADBOY had his way, this would end before sundown tomorrow night somewhere in a closed vicinity off of Ontario Street.

It had gone and for long enough between he and David Dane, a relationship spanning two decades that had seen Markem train Dane, become his mentor, his house mate, and even his hero.

Now, alone in the quiet confines of a hotel room, THE MONARCH OF THE MARITIMES, THE RICO SUAVE BADBOY, as well as the man who was once known as "HOLLYWOOD" for his incredible looks would plot the destruction of his protégé who had become world famous, that, and Paris and Barclay would get a crack at the legendary and iconic, Robert and Richard Gray.

Eddy for some reason had absconded, strangely enough having a bout of conscience. Suddenly, he seemed to feel some type of remorse for what he had decided to become a part of. There was no accounting for other peoples judgement, and you couldn't legislate brains. It was a free world, or free enough, you had to go with the flow. They were like a pack of wolves who were finally hungry enough to seek out and destroy their prey, with or without Eddy Dorozowsky.

"Where's Jack"?? Chris asked in his customary rough voice.

"I don't know". Barclay said. "Scott saw him earlier on down in the lobby. I think he was at the bar drinking with some girl".

"Go find him and tell him that we're gonna go to the gym and do some training. I wanna be at my best when I finally show the world who the real celebrity is". Markem remarked.

"I'll go look for him". Paris replied.

Just then, Chris's phone lit up as he looked down at the screen on the call display. "That's Gregory like. I wonder what he wants". Markem pondered quizzically.

Gregory was Chris and Jacks younger Brother, there were seven boys in all.

"We should be back next week". Chris explained to his younger sibling who was also known for his physical capabilities as a street fighter. The entire Family was dangerous, with Chris, Jack, and Gregory taking up the lead as the hardest and the strongest. There were also four sisters.

"I'll be out back in five. Tell Jack to meet us". Chris said to Scott who was standing by the door. "And get room service to bring up some towels. We've been out since last night" … … … … … … … …

SEXXXY EDDY stepped into THE BLACK DOMINO TAVERN wearing a red parka over black jeans as he approached "THE IMMORTAL" VON "THE ICON" who was sitting on the other side of the room with ROBERT AND RICHARD GRAY flanking him as bodyguards would their client.

"Why are you here"?? VON asked looking up at EDDY from his seated position. There was sunlight filtering in through the window in the side door to the left of where he was sitting with a bewildered grin on his face.

RICHARD and ROBERT were not smiling.

"For exactly the reason that I should've been here all along. Chris and Jack Markem are coming for you very, very, soon". He said. "Your teacher wants to prove that he's the real superstar of the two of you. He's planning to make an example out of you".

"He didn't need to go to these lengths to prove that. I would've agreed with that minus the urging". VON said twisting a straw at both ends between the thumb and fore finger of either hand as he sat slightly back in a plastic lawn chair, feet slightly elevated on a wooden stoop.

"Apparently, that's not good enough for him. He wants the entire world to see him put on a show".

Just then the front door to the bar opened and a familiar face wandered in.

The fuck's he still doing in town?? VON wondered as Damian The Dealer strolled toward him.

"Why are you here"?? VON reinforced with respect to Eddy.

"Because getting mad and turning on someone completely are two different things. I'm not gonna assist them in your demise".

Dane was perplexed now.

"You shouldn't even be in town at this point". "THE IMMORTAL" VON "THE ICON" remarked shooting a sharp glance in Damians direction.

"I know, but when I heard what was about to happen, I decided to stay. Word travels fast around here".

"How the fuck did you hear what was about to happen"?? VON questioned with extreme curiosity

"Because a stripper who's a friend of mine was in Chris Markems hotel room, she overheard the whole conversation that they were having. I've talked about you a hundred times so she knew your name right off the bat. It's not like her memory had to be refreshed". He said.

"I think that Chris is gonna end up being out numbered". Robert commented.

"I'm sorry bro". EDDY said to his long time friend. There was a tear in his eye.

"I don't know if that's good enough". Richard scolded.

"It probably shouldn't be". EDDY apologized.

Dane took stock of his old friend for a moment. It had always been in his nature to forgive. "Alright, but there won't be another shot. This is it". THE IMMORTAL ONE said.

"Let's go". VON said raising from his seat and quickly embracing SEXXXY EDDY who genuinely had a change of heart.

"Let's give em Hell". He said seriously.

As darkness fell over Ontario Street, THE IMMORTAL VON "THE ICON" stood in the posture of a Texas Ranger as he waited anxiously for his mentor and his entourage to show up in the back alley that had been agreed upon hours ago.

"I've waited twenty years for this". Chris Markem said at David Danes back as points of light from the overhead vapour lamps extended and then burnt off in the surreal bluish darkness that now engulfed both sets of camp members.

On VON "THE ICON"'S side there was KATE "THE GATE" SHAMROCK, SEXXXY EDDY, and ROBERT AND RICHARD GRAY. On CHRIS MARKEMS side, there was JACK MARKEM, SCOTT PARIS, TROY BARCLAY, and two bodybuilders that VON had never seen before in his life.

"There's no need for us to do this. I don't wanna do this". Dane said staring into the smouldering eyes of THE RICO SUAVE BADBOY who had trained him, cradled him, brought him along, and even mentored him. This was the scariest experience of David Danes life. No turning back, terror inside, and enough butterflies to go around.

Markem had taught him everything that he knew. He was supposed to be THE RICO SUAVE BADBOYS successor, although Dane knew that he could never, and would never be able to live up to the legend who trained him.

There were dangerous men on both sides. This could get very unholy very fast.

"You gave me every skill that I have. I can never out match you".

Markem was smirking lightly, his skills boasted far more accolades than did David Danes did.

"You're gonna be better off after tonight like. There's one more lesson to be learned". Markem said swinging at the center of David Danes nose and connecting as a collective WHOOOA!!! Swooped violently over the crowd as blood began to flow from VON "THE ICONS" nostrils.

"Kill em Uncle VON"!!! KATE yelled with venom in her eyes.

"Fuck you"!!! THE IMMORTAL one answered delivering three consecutive jabs followed by a powerful left hook aimed at the man who trained him. Hit with bad intentions, that's what Markem had taught him.

"Cmon like Chris"!!! Jack hollered as his Brother nailed a left jab followed by a right cross that dropped David Dane to his knees.

"Cmon DANE, GET UP"!!! ROBERT GRAY hollered searing a hole through Chris Markems soul with an intense glare.

Dane brought his wrist up between Markems legs giving himself just enough time to return to his feet only for Chris Markem to take him down again using a technique from his Greco Roman Wrestling days.

"Close the guard Uncle Von!!! Improve the position"!!! Kate yelled as Von twisted his mentor into a rear naked choke that he had seen Canadian Legend Bret Hart use in the past.

"Squeeze VON"!!! SEXXXY EDDY yelled as he gestured with both of his hands.

Markem had rolled out and stood up, back on both feet now throwing punches, left, right, left, as Dane for the most part ducked and stayed out of his way.

"You can stop this anytime". ONTARIO STREETS PRODIGAL SON shouted.

Luigi was somewhere in the back ground shooting footage of what was transpiring.

"How, you, doin"?? Markem signatured striking his student with a wicked left hook that's affects would be felt for days.

"Jab Dane"!!! RICHARD hollered from the sidelines as Jack looked his way and smirked menacingly.

"You want a crack at us"?? ROBERT asked glaring, hard stare, at Troy Barclay. "Over here"!!! The African/Canadian Bodybuilder invited as VON shouldered MARKEM back first into a chain link fence.

The blood was free flowing now, here, there, everywhere and both mens eyes were swelling up.

Markem was dancing backward now, sticking and moving and Dane was reeling.

"Cmon Uncle VON. Kill this arrogant motherfucker"!!! Kate shouted as ROBERT GRAY floored Scott Paris with an open handed slap across the head sending him to the pavement.

VON was returning fire now jabbing for all he was worth, rapid fire, three and then one. Three jabs and then a left. Most people only threw two. Chris had himself taught his student that.

"You're going right through that white picket fence"!!! Markem shouted charging at Dane like a cruise missile. His shirt was off, over his head now, and his perspiring torso was glistening over black leather pants and white sneakers.

RICHARD GRAY and TROY BARCLAY were trading punches in the blue hew that the night sky was providing several feet away. There was blood dripping from everywhere on both their faces now as ROBERT lifted PARIS nearby and slammed him onto the hood of a TRANS-AM that a local owned.

VON had stepped away and Markem had gone forehead first through the fence and was split wide across the temple now, gushing red fluid all over.

"GET UP"!!! VON yelled as Markem rose to his feet and charged violently in the direction of his protégé again this time taking him into the ground where both men would stay down for the count with neither student nor teacher being able to continue.

On the other side of the night RICHARD and ROBERT were still busy trading blows with SCOTT PARIS and TROY BARCLAY who were fighting back with everything that they had in them.

"What's wrong man"?? ROBERT GRAY asked pissed enough to drink blood.

"OOH, DID THAT HURT"??!!!!! RICHARD asked ground slamming TROY BARCLAY who was no longer able to do anything but moan and hold his rib cage, veiny eyed, and done.

"I have one more statement to make"!!! ROBERT said hitting Scott Paris so hard that he spun around before falling head first to the concrete, unconscious, finished, last call … … … … … … … …

"You did good like David. I'm proud of you". Markem said rising, unaided to his feet and wrapping his arms around his bloodied student. "That was your final lesson like". THE LEGENDARY RICO SUAVE BADBOY said lifting his battered and beaten student to his feet.

"Now you've learned all that I have to teach you". Markem said in his typical, don't do as I do, do as I say, hard ass fashion. He was a legend for a reason.

"I love you kid". Chris said as THE IMMORTAL VON "THE ICON" stabilized himself. "I love you to". He said. "I love you to". Both men traded as they embraced one another in the oily, glistening, Ontario Street night that was fueled by sweat, labored breathing, and a life time of memories.

Kate was crying on the sidelines and Jack was smiling emotionally now. "Ah … … … … Chris, he'll teach him one way or another like. That's just his way". The kick boxer said warmly. He had always loved his Brothers student, and so had his Brother, this was just Chris Markems hard ass, take no prisoners way of showing it. "Good for you you like". Jack said embracing Dane as he walked to the sidelines.

"Thanks Jack"!!! VON "THE ICON" said with blood pouring from his forehead.

Dane felt as though the crimson ground below was rising up to meet him.

One more ONTARIO STREET NIGHT had come to a close … … … … … … … … … …

CHRIS AND JACK -This is the part of the book where I speak to you both directly. First of all, to the man who trained me, CHRIS POOLE, THE REAL RICO SUAVE BAD BOY. I couldn't lay a glove on you nor Uncle Jack as I will always think of him. You are both my heroes.

Chris, If it weren't for the hours and hours of training that you bestowed upon me, I wouldn't be able to take care of myself as well as I can today, in the ring, or outside of it. You will always be my coach, my hero, my friend, and my mentor. I love you, no matter what.

Once upon a time you referred to me as "A product of you". I'm proud of that honor, and of being your successor, for me, you always gave COOL a whole new meaning from your style, down to your ability to take care of yourself in the street and elsewhere. There is no other like you, truly.

The storyline presented in this book is solely for the purposes of entertainment, and I know that you're comfortable playing The Bad Guy. "Women, tend to like The Rico Suave BADBOY like David". I remember you once saying with a cigarette dangling from your lips as you reached for a light. You were sitting in front of the window of our apartment in

Vancouver. Those days and night so many years ago, both in Hali and in Vancouver, will last forever.

There's a song that played in the bars in Vancouver by sound Garden that makes me think of when we were out in B.C. That's why I'll always think of those days and nights as what happened under The Black Hole Sun.

I miss you dude,
Alright, take care.
Your Friend and Student … … … … Von.

PART III

THE OTHER SIDE OF DARKNESS

NOVEMBER 7th, 2015-MONICA- I miss you Baby Bunny. Today marks the third anniversary of your death. I'd give all of my tomorrows to hold you one more time and remember our million and one days and nights under Ontario Streets black skies that melted into fiery hued dawns. My memories of you are timeless. You are the most special person who has ever come into my life aside from my beautiful niece Kate. There will never be another you, ever.

    R.I.P.   MONICA   MEDEIROS   ABBONA-Eternal Life … … … … … … … … … … … …

When VON "THE ICON" awoke the next morning Robert and Richard had left town and returned to Nova Scotia. There was now a sense of calm within him in terms of the way that Ontario Streets most popular and iconic legend felt about the way that everything had worked out. He had made it through another adventure alive, and lived to tell the tale.

In his minds eye, he saw Lilly Chicoine ascending a flight of stone steps toward a statue that was shrouded in white smoke as if out of a dream, its platform littered with orange leaves and scattered foliage that seemed to stir ever so slightly as if made from fantasy.

Today, November 7th, was the anniversary of her fatal accident on Highway 403. It was the worst tragedy that David Dane had ever been forced to endure. He had lost the one human being on this planet aside from Kate who was far more important to him than his own existence on this planet.

Somewhere dust settled in the universe as the grill of Lillys Nissan Maxima flashed horrifically behind David Danes eyes like an image sent from a far off nightmare before fading back to the dawn of the present and the fabric of the red sheets of his bed.

"Uncle Von". A voice echoed from the other side of his bedroom door.

"Yeah". He answered reaching for a black T-shirt that was hanging on a chair below the window.

"Can I come in"?? Kate asked.

"Sure".

As the door came open, VON immediately noticed Kates somber demeanour as she came to sit on the edge of his mattress and put her arms around him. "I know what day today is, and I know that of all days of the year this isn't the easiest".

There were tears streaking VON "THE ICONS" cheeks now as he fought to answer his nieces words. "Yeah, you can say that again". He said quickly.

"We all know how much you loved her. She couldn't have asked for a better boyfriend. You love her eternally. Not many girls can say they ever knew a love like that".

"Yeah". VON responded vaguely as he wiped a tear that had made it half way down his left cheek.

"You need to get out today. Maybe we can go visit Lilly's grave". She said.

"Thanks Kate". VON said turning his head slightly to glance in the direction of the shadowy venetian blinds that masked the windows view.

On the other side of town SEXXXY EDDY was dropping a card in a red mailbox that said "CANADA POST" on the side. Its context read'
HEY VON,
   I know what day today is buddy. I just wanted you to know
   That I'm thinking of you. You were the best boyfriend and husband
   That she could've asked for.
   Be in touch soon.
   SEX ED

As David Dane rose from his bed he headed toward the window of his bedroom and gently touched the rain soaked window with the tips of his fingers. He had had the experience of his life because of the woman known as Lilly" BAD TO THE BONE" Chicoine. She had provided the inspiration for three books as well as given him a name around the world. There was only one, and there would never again be another. She was, as her nickname suggested, BAD TO THE BONE!!!

As Von stepped out of his room and into the dimly lit shadows at the front of the house he found Marilyn Dane standing in front of a sparsely bleeding goose neck lamp in the shadows of the rain. There was a gun in her hand. Her mascara had run, and her hand was trembling.

There was a black ski mask with the eye holes cut out of it lying on the desk top.

Kate was standing motionless in front of her, as if she had been stricken of her ability to move.

"Nana did it. She's the one who shot those people on the beach". She said meekly.

Danes face was like stone now, but before he could say anything Marilyn lifted the barrel of the gun to her temple, uttered the words "Goodbye", and pulled the trigger.

"NOOO"!!! VON hollered as he watched blood from her skull spatter onto the wall across from them.

"She said that we took her place as CANADIAN HEROES and that the shooting in Old Montreal was in the name of her flag". Kate said throwing her arms around her Uncle.

Marilyn had been born in Scotland, and moved to Canada as an immigrant at ten years old.

So, this thing ends the same way that it began, with us, THE ONTARIO STREET ORIGINAL ORIGINALS.

And to MONICA, my love for all of eternity. I will never let you down. I'll see you on the other side of darkness.

God Bless You Forever,
VON

THE END!!!

Please stay tuned for The Class Of 2015, Ontario Street Hall Of Fame … … … … … … … … … … … … … …

MONICA-Before this book ever went to press I made the conscious decision that you deserved to be Re-Inducted into the O.S.H.O.F. under your own name. I also want to be crystal clear that you are still the FIRST EVER INDUCTEE into THE ONTARIO STREET HALL OF FAME despite the re-induction under your given name. I also had to struggle with the decision as to whether or not to prepare another speech or simply reprint the old one. So, here's what I came up with.

What I've decided to do is to present a shorter, somewhat, para-phrased version of your original induction. I hope that's okay with you Baby Bunny. I'll always love you. I'll see you in Heaven.

MONICA- I'll always think of you as The Street Angel that I met in the millennium. You, aside from my niece Kate are the most special person who has ever walked into my life, and that's exactly what you did on that dark and rainy afternoon such a long time ago. Getting to know you was like nothing else that's ever happened to me. You were always an enigma, from your unique one of a kind personality to the dark and exclusive world that you came from. You gave me the experience of my life, you were an experience.

You are the private dancer in my dreams, and the legend that I long to hold one more time. My life has never been the same without you in it. Whether now, or in a thousand years, I'll hold onto your memory forever.

I induct you, MONICA MEDEIROS ABBONA, into THE CLASS OF 2015, ONTARIO STREET HALL OF FAME!!!

HALL OF FAME BY THE SCRIPT PLAYS OVER THE LOUD SPEAKERS!!!

My next Inductee is a unique individual with his very own set of characteristics. He walks on all fores, eats Hypoallergenic Dog Food, and has the kindest, softest, most gentle heart of any K-9 that I've ever known aside from my late, great, Sheppard, Lab, Collie, mix, HUNTER.

We were first introduced to each other on adoption day at The S.P.C.A.

When I first saw him, I thought that he was the most intimidating looking animal that I'd ever seen. I didn't bond with him right away. Over the next several weeks I wrestled with the realization that I was so afraid of him that I didn't know whether or not I'd be able to keep him, and that he may be better off with someone else.

It wasn't until I saw him in a hundred different situations that I finally came to the realization that he was as harmless as a child, and had a genuinely special and loving character. We've gone for a thousand walks in Old Montreal and strolled the water front in the summertime, walked for miles from one end of ONTARIO STREET to another and back again. We've been to Mount Royal, Sherbrook West, and even a few places that we call our own which I won't list here.

In the days, nights, and months that followed we became the very best of friends.

There is no other animal out there like him.

So, I now Induct, my constant companion, and very best friend, WARRIOR, into THE CLASS OF 2015, ONTARIO STREET HALL OF FAME … … … … … … … … … … … …

HALL OF FAME BY THE SCRIPT BLASTS ON AS SPOTLIGHTS SWOON AND A STATUE IN THE SHAPE OF A DOGO IS PRESENTED … … … … … … … … … … … … … … … … …

IN MEMORY OF MONICA MEDEIROS ABBONA-JANUARY 5th, 1978 to NOVEMBER 7th, 2012

LOVE ALWAYS

Printed in the United States
By Bookmasters